HOT BLOOD

Also by John Burton Thompson

Born to be Made
Kiss or Kill
One More for the Road
Swamp Nymph
The Girls of the French Quarter

HOT BLOOD

JOHN BURTON THOMPSON

CUTTING EDGE

ISBN-13: 978-1-952138-65-2

Published by
Cutting Edge Books
PO Box 8212
Calabasas, CA 91372
www.cuttingedgebooks.com

CHAPTER ONE

THE GIRL was speaking, her face serious and frightened. "Jerry, you shouldn't have come. You know what Grandfather said he'd do if he caught you here again. He might come back at any minute."

The boy smiled, his white teeth flashing in the shadowy sunlight of the arbor. "Who cares what the old goat says? I wanted to see you, so I came. God, but you're beautiful!"

She smiled and sank into a rough, canvas-covered lounge, the favorite resting place of her grandfather when he was preparing a sermon.

"Do you really think so, Jerry?"

Jerry did, and his avid eyes devoured her slender length from her daintily slim ankles upward past the fine sculpture of her calves and thighs to her small waist and eagerly erect breasts that surged against the cloth of her simple dress as though seeking sudden exit. Her face was calm and enigmatic, a beautiful placid face, so delicately assembled that it had a stirring, ethereal purity. Her eyes were a deep sea-green and her hair a mass of soft gunmetal black, luxuriously shining about her head like a smoky halo. As she indolently lay back on the cushions, long thick lashes shaded her eyes with that age-old provocation that has been a man-trap since the days of Mother Eve. Jerry Booth was a man despite his young years, and his throat constricted, his palms growing damp and hot. With a sudden movement, he sat beside her.

"What do I care about your grandfather or anyone else?" he asked huskily. "Karel, I love you."

1

Her breasts heaved as her breathing grew faster. Jerry was unconventional, exciting. He had traveled widely, and to her young mind he represented all the things she had dreamed of but had never experienced or seen. That his parents were shiftless and little more than traveling beggars mattered to her even less than his manifest poverty. Jerry was handsome and dark, and his eyes laughed all the time. If his pants were patched and his shirt threadbare, he was clean and managed to lend his mean clothing a part of his own personable charm so that one forgot them— especially if one was young, starved for affection and dominated by a stern scripture-quoting grandfather.

His nearness intoxicated her mind and, though a strident inner voice shouted at her in warning, the delicious rigor that the touch of his hands induced set up a clamor much louder and far more irresistible. She could see him dimly as he pulled her slowly toward him, his hands sliding across her back and setting up almost unendurable trails of sensation that both attracted and shocked her. She could feel his breath on her cheek and, though the voice warned her again, she could scarcely hear it.

"Jerry," her voice was weak and his name on her lips was nei-ther resistance nor entreaty. It was only a soft sigh that seemed to admit the inevitable. His lips closed over hers and a surge of hot blood went through her in a burning wave. Karel had stolen kisses at odd moments in chance fortuitous places, but nothing like this had ever happened to her before. So heady was the touch of his tongue on hers that she almost swooned, and the electrify-ing sensation that started up her leg made her lithe, elastic body react to the call of a newly fledged urgency. She could sense its sinuous progress while tension and demand built up in her like the waters of a suddenly dammed stream. She put out a hand to stop him but it made contact with his and their fingers inter-twined greedily. Her shuddering whimpers were muffled only by the devouring efforts of their lips mouthing together.

Suddenly she moved her head away, looking at him through large, glazed eyes. "Oh … Jerry!" Her arms went around him and, holding him in a grip of steel, she sank back on the rough canvas, any last vestige of resistance dissolving under Nature's most penetrating drive.

Across the fence, old Dr. Theodore Franchette, his grizzled brow dripping with sweat that had nothing to do with the heat of the day, turned carefully away and walked back toward his own house. His only aim was to reach his study, close the door to the rest of the world and give serious attention to the scene he had just witnessed.

As he went up the front steps, Maude Franchette, her solid, comfortable bulk firmly ensconced in a wicker rocking chair on the porch, took her eyes from her knitting just long enough to note his troubled face and air of consternation. Her gentle rocking neither increased nor decreased. She was complacent, imperturbable and long accustomed to the unpredictable ups and downs of her volatile, brilliant husband. He glowered down at her for a moment.

"You," he barked, "are a woman and, therefore, supposed to possess the wisdom of the ages. Sometimes I don't think any of you have the brains of a flea, but right now I'll take the chance that maybe you can muster up one tiny morsel of good sense. Maybe you can tell me what on earth to do when you see other people head their lives straight for hell—straight for the worst kind of unhappiness—when they don't even know they're doing it?"

Maude knitted and rocked. "Well," she said, "it seems to me that would depend."

"Don't qualify!" he roared. "I knew I could depend on you to hedge. That's where you women are always so smart. You never come out in the open."

"Suppose you tell me just who is headed for this downward descent?"

"Karel Snowden is, that's who. And that grandfather of hers is the whole cause—that driveling, sniveling, parboiled old hypocrite, Rathborne."

Maude raised her eyebrows. She, too, was interested in Karel, partly because she had been fond of Karel's mother and partly because she pitied anyone subject to the Reverend Rathborne's domination and influence. He was widely believed to have driven his daughters away from home at an early age because of his unendurable discipline. There were other rumors, too, so ugly that no one in Kenton had ever wanted to believe them. Maude wholly shared her husband's views of the Reverend, and she knew also that the man's discipline was for others, never for himself, for he fondly believed that his own moral peculations were deeply hidden and secret.

"In what particular way is Karel headed for such unhappiness?" she asked.

The Doctor moved his chin, making his spade beard teeter like a sandpiper. "I was an unwilling witness to a bit of love-making today. Ordinarily I'm all in favor of young people and their … er … when they … well, I'm all in favor of it, but this time—I don't know."

"You are being very cryptic."

The little man ran thin, sensitive fingers through raven black hair and sighed. "Do you know the Booths?"

"You mean those gypsy sort of people that put up in that cabin on the Patterson place?"

He nodded vigorously. "The same. Well, the boy has taken it on himself to nurture a terrific crush on Karel. The girl has been starved for affection and one can hardly blame her for anything she does to get it, but Rathborne has threatened to horsewhip the boy if he catches him around again."

Maude clucked her lips and sighed. "That's too bad."

"What is?" he demanded with a bird-like jerk of his head.

She shrugged. "Oh—the situation, the probable unhappiness, and you right in the middle of it, as always. You and Fannie Blumendahl."

"This is one time when Fannie Blumendahl can stay put and watch. I'm going to handle this all by myself."

"Are you?"

"What do you mean by that?" he asked suspiciously.

"Nothing. You made a statement and I asked you if you meant it."

"I meant it," he replied doggedly. "Aren't you interested in what I saw today?"

"Of course I am. I knew you'd get around to telling it eventually."

He glowered affectionately at her and took a cheroot from his pocket, bit off the end and lit it. "Well, I was pulling a caterpillar nest out of that Stuart pecan tree back there on our boundary where it butts up against Rathborne's back fence and ..."

When he had finished speaking, Maude sat silently, her rocking ceased.

"So there you are," he said, gnawing at his cheroot. "A thing like that can only lead to unhappiness."

"I agree," she said pensively, "but I'd like to know your reasons. Why only to unhappiness?"

He grew excited again. "In the first place, the boy is no good. He's a complete wastrel, a tramp and a nobody. Mind you, now, I'm no snob. If he wanted to make a place in the world for himself and Karel and if I was certain he loved her, I'd put out a hand to help in a second. But I'm assured of none of this. In the second place, Rathborne is bound to cause trouble. He's nothing but an ass and an abomination. He's worse off, as far as I'm concerned, than a lot of people in the asylum at Jackson who have been taken forcibly from society. He's a madman and a hazard to everyone around him."

"One would think that you thought very little of him."

"In that respect one could hardly be more correct. I even resent the fact that the man uses up his quota of God's air."

"But he is a man of God," said Maude sententiously.

Dr. Franchette said a very ungentlemanly word and almost swallowed the butt of his cheroot. "If that is true, then I charge God with a serious error of judgment. He is certainly lacking in discrimination and good taste."

"That," said Maude in gentle rebuke, "is blasphemy."

The Doctor let go a furious grunt and faced her with glaring conviction in his eyes. "I still say there's unhappiness ahead and I deplore it. I hate it worse than I do any disease because for most diseases there are at least drugs that can be used. But for this—what?" He threw up his hands.

Maude slowly picked up her knitting. "The child is a neighbor. She is young and she has been shamefully mistreated. True, for diseases there are drugs. And for this oncoming case of unhappiness, there is Theodore Franchette—Cajun-American, M. D., retired—and Fannie Blumendahl. Don't be a fool and try to freeze Fannie out of it."

The Reverened Charles Peckham Rathborne was a tall, spare man whose austere face seemed to have been scoured free of any excess flesh, leaving its gray skin taut and stretched over the bridge of his sharp nose and shrunken into the cavernous hollows under his high cheek bones. His lips were bloodless and dry and covered, with tight precision, a set of store-bought, yellowed teeth. His large, coal-dark eyes burned fiercely with the fire of a true fanatic.

He entered his house and placed his hat on a spindly table under a mirror long since clouded over. The only sound was that of silence, and a musty pall of gloom clung shroud-like to every corner. He dusted off his lapels absently and walked down the narrow, dark hall toward the dining room. It was time for lunch and Rathborne was a meticulous man about punctuality, especially when it concerned others.

The dining room was vacant and the mean little stove in the kitchen showed that no cooking had been done since breakfast. He compressed his lips into a thin, straight line and went in search of his granddaughter. She was not in the house and, after a thorough search of all the likely places in the yard, he finally reached the scuppernong arbor. There she lay on the old canvas couch, lost in a dimly conscious daydream, her body displayed gracefully and a smooth, ivory-tan thigh bare to his eyes.

"Karel!"

She rolled over, gasping and pulling her dress down. "Yes, sir?"

"I wish to be informed of your purpose in lying there in that disgraceful attitude, with your dress half off. Holy Father preserve us! Your underthings—off! Completely off!" His face turned a muddy crimson and he picked them up gingerly, holding them out before him as though they were dirty and offensive. His eyes were burning wells of outrage.

"What," he hissed, "is the meaning of this? Answer me— answer me!"

In spite of her predicament, in spite of fear of what he might do, the girl could not immediately overcome her dreamy lassitude, her feeling of complete bodily well-being and peace. Her eyes were drowsy, the lids as smooth as a polished pearl. Her face, though somewhat concerned and anxious, still wore a sheen of placid repleteness, of unutterable satiation.

As he watched, waiting for her to speak, the reason for her appearance struck him with the impact of a hard-driven fist. He turned pale and his breath caught in his throat.

"It was that Jerry Booth, wasn't it? Answer me. I say—*answer me!*" He raised his hand and stood over her like the avenging angel. Still lethargic and dull, stunned and half-hypnotized by his frenzied utterances, she nodded dumbly. The arm went down and a crackling slap resounded from her smooth cheek. She turned away with a cry, trying to escape the hard, bony fingers as they beat her across the head and face.

Five minutes later, sobbing wretchedly through swollen, bleeding lips, she allowed him to assist her to the house. Straight to her bedroom he took her, his eyes burning feverishly and his stiff hair standing wildly on end. He hurled her into a chair and called her a name that has caused women to blanch and shrink since the dawn of history.

The girl huddled in the chair, sobbing, her face cradled protectively in her arms.

"I take you," he stormed, "a child of my own daughter—may her festering soul rot in hell till the end of time—I take you and I give you a good home. I give you a God-fearing atmosphere, protection, the best of everything, and the first tramp that pays you a little attention you give yourself away to—just as your mother gave herself to that worthless heretic in the Godforsaken union that produced you. God's will be done, however, and she did not survive to bring more like you into the world. Stand up and disrobe. I am a fair and just man. I will see your guilt for myself."

She raised her head. "No—no!" His hand descended once more and her head snapped back from the force of the blow.

"I will know!" he screamed, his eyes shining insanely. "I will know. I will save you from the fires of hell, Karel. I will, I tell you. Stand before me and expose your guilt!" Again he struck her with brutal force.

Like an automaton, she pulled herself from the chair and stripped the dress over her head. Her quaking hands fumbled with her slip, and with an animal-like sound, he stripped it from her in tatters.

"I will know!" he chanted repeatedly. "I will know!"

Finally she stood naked before him, shrinking, making a half-hearted attempt to cover herself.

"Never you mind the modesty now," he rasped. "Stand straight and put your arms down." She did so and his eyes roved gluttonously over the divine sculpture of her body—hotly, raven-ously he gazed. He passed a trembling hand over his eyes and then raised them to heaven. "Guide me, oh Lord. Guide me and tell me wherein lies my duty."

Commencing a sonorous prayer that lasted fifteen minutes, he called upon God to witness the purity of his efforts to put her on the right road, putting the blame for her dastardly actions on the meanness of her parentage and the polluted blood that ran in her veins. He stopped, panting for breath, his face a deathly yellow and in his eyes a mad, unearthly light. Approaching her, he ran his hands over her shoulders and down her soft, trembling flanks.

"It is right," he muttered. "It is right and only by a man of God can the touch of a man of the devil be erased."

With awful strength he drew her close and mouthed the peaks of her breasts with his rough lips. She began to struggle, the breath stopping in her throat, her head swimming and her muscles turned to milk. His hands roved over her and, mouthing incoherencies that had to do with cleansing and driving out the devil, he bore her backward to the bed. Her senses reeled and her struggles grew weaker and weaker, whimpering cries coming from her lips as her head went back on the rough counterpane in a last, despairing effort.

When she regained consciousness, her grandfather was kneeling by the bed in prayer, his eyes closed, his lips parched and dry. She almost fainted again, and her limp muscles refused to move at her bidding. As his prayer drew to a close, he rose to his feet and looked down at her through cold, distant eyes.

"You will now prepare my lunch. God approves of what I have done. The answer has come through clearly." She looked at him uncomprehendingly. "And so that the sinful union between you and that Booth boy shall reap no more like either of you—soulless, hell-bent heretics—I shall perform my charitable duty and enlist the forces of medical science without delay."

Thirty minutes later Dr. Franchette answered his doorbell and gazed at his visitor with undisguised dislike. "You wanted something?"

The Reverend Rathborne nodded. "I hesitated to approach you, Theodore, because I am aware that you are not disposed to be friendly with me. Naturally, since you are of Catholic inclinations—"

"For your information, I am not a Catholic," the Doctor replied stiffly. "And even if I were, it would have nothing to do with my feelings toward you which you have just described so accurately but incompletely."

Rathborne shrugged indifferently. "I find myself faced with the odious task of coming to you for help. It has to do with another and I find that, though I am a doctor of souls, I am not a doctor of bodies."

"That bit of belated wisdom must have shocked your sensitive spirit no end," suggested the little man caustically.

"I am immune to your sarcasm, Theodore," murmured the Minister. "May I come in and sit down?"

"I suppose common courtesy bids it. Which one of your flock is ill? My son can handle the case for you. He is the active member of the family now."

"I have every respect for Albert's abilities as a physician," said the other. "This, however, has to do with Karel, and knowing that she worships you above all men, I thought that for her sake you might drop your dislike of me for the moment and advise me."

Dr. Franchette sat down suddenly, feeling that his prophecy of unhappiness had fledged with upsetting abruptness. "If it has to do with Karel, proceed by all means."

"She," said Rathborne, building an unlovely steeple with his bony hands, "accomplished an assignation with that wretched Booth boy today."

The Doctor felt a sudden, sharp pain in his stomach but managed to retain a calm visage. "Indeed, and how do you know that?"

"I found her in the arbor on that old couch where I study and devise sermons. She was in a very odd position and seemed only about half conscious. Her underdrawers were hard by in a state of dishevelment. I made her admit to everything."

"First your own daughter and now your granddaughter. Rathborne, I warn you, don't ever place yourself in my hands medically. I have taken an oath which means a great deal to me, having to do with the sayings of Hippocrates regarding medical ethics. You are the only man I ever knew who might make me break it. If you had some malady that called for bicarbonate of soda, I doubt that I could resist substituting prussic acid."

The Minister sat suddenly straight. "Do I understand you to imply that the fault is—*mine*?"

"You do," snapped the Doctor, "unless your understanding has atrophied along with the rest of you."

"I'm afraid," said Rathborne getting to his feet, "that I am wasting my time here."

"You have wasted all the rest of it," said the other with hostility. "Why be inconsistent? You are a fool, Rathborne, a fool of such herculean stature that it would be worse than useless to attempt to reason with you. The very best thing that could possibly happen to Karel would be for you to break your neck as you go down my front steps. You won't, of course, and humanity will go right on suffering—Karel more than the rest."

Rathborne looked at the Doctor with contemptuous hauteur. "I bid you good afternoon, Theodore. Pray forgive me for intruding upon you and taking up your time."

"Are you going to horsewhip young Booth?" asked Franchette with sly malice.

"I am certainly going to see that he is punished."

"I was hoping you'd try that horsewhipping stunt you speak of so often. I think the boy would probably beat you within an inch of your life. I should like to be there to see all of it and then salt and pepper your wounds." With a sniff, the other turned about and walked through the door.

"You have made an enemy," said Maude as she padded into the study. "Here's your coffee."

The little man stirred sugar and cream into the dark, strong brew. "I never in my life was so moved to murder a man."

Maude sat down and stirred her own cup of coffee. "And in the meantime, that poor child lives in a hell twice done over now that he knows. Where is this vaunted fixitiveness that you and Fannie are always bragging about?"

He pounded the desk with a slow beat. "Maude, I am so determined to put this thing right that I can't seem to think of what should be done short of murdering the old bastard."

"You're being silly now," she said as she sipped the hot coffee slowly. "You know very well you're not going to murder anyone."

"I'm so mad I could," he fumed, fumbling for a cheroot. He found it and bit at the end viciously. "As I was saying—"

The door of the office burst open and Karel ran to him and fell sobbing into his arms. She clung to him with desperate strength as though afraid ever to let him go. He tried to quiet her but she wept harder and began to shake uncontrollably. Her body went into a hard convulsion and her lips became flecked with froth. "Brandy, Maude," he said brusquely. "And a hypo—luminal."

By main strength he disengaged her and drew his hand back to slap her but he suddenly saw the ugly hand marks raising to purple and swollen welts on her face. He grasped her by the shoulders and shook her, but to little avail. Maude returned with a small glass of brandy, a filled hypo and a wet towel. He seized the towel and slapped Karel stingingly across the face several times. She subsided into a shuddering huddle of abject misery on the floor, her face slack, her eyes unseeing and blank. He made her drink the brandy and then gave her a shot in the arm. Twenty minutes later she lay on Maude's bed, quiet save for occasional twitching, and told them a story that came within an inch of shaking Maude's rock-like aplomb. Dr. Franchette was sweating freely when she finished.

"That's enough talking, my dear," he said in a voice that was gentle but firm. "Sleep a while now."

"I'm never going back!" She sat up in bed, panic-stricken. "I'm not going back—I can't! Oh God, if he ever touches me again, I'll kill him! I know I will." She started sobbing again and the old man took her into his arms and let her cry.

"You sleep now," he said. "We'll think of something."

Out in the hall Maude placed her own stamp upon what he had just said. "You certainly had *better* think of something."

It was nearly five that afternoon when the minister made his second appearance of the day. "I'm not here to intrude upon your time, Doctor," he said without preamble. "I am looking for my granddaughter."

"Why?"

"I beg your pardon?"

"What do you want with her? Do you want to rape her again?"

The man turned the color of whey. "How dare you make such an accusation? How dare you! How—"

"Shut up. She's here and in a state of nervous collapse. My inclination, Rathborne, is to shoot you like a mad dog. I knew you were vicious in your own misguided way but I had no idea you would attack your own blood, and in the name of 'purifying' her. Where did you ever get such insane poppycock?"

"You'll answer for that accusation, Theodore Franchette—in a court of law. This is not the last of it between us by any means. Where is she? I have come to take her home."

"You will do no such thing," shot back the Doctor. "I have said that she is in a dangerous condition and cannot be moved. She stays, and just you try to get her."

"I'll get a court order. I'll accuse you of kidnapping."

Franchette laughed. "Just try it. It would be a good popularity contest, if nothing else. You'd see pretty quick that you're a dead duck in this town."

"Then you refuse to turn her over to me."

"I most certainly do refuse."

The man's eyes blazed dementedly as he stood on the porch, his ruff of hair standing wildly on end. He then turned swiftly about and with long strides walked down the brick path.

"What'll he do now?" asked Maude.

"I don't know. I know what I'm going to do though. I'm going to take her to the Clinic. He might well point out that, if she's that badly done-in, she should be in a place designed to take care of the ill. Call Albert and tell him to send the ambulance along. That'll put a crimp in your man of God."

That night just before supper his daughter-in-law, Lisabeth, ran into his office and plopped into his lap. "Hi, Dad," she said, planting a moist kiss on his cheek.

"Go on—git. I'm in no mood for horseplay. I'm trying to think and you come bustin' in and destroy my train of thought. Go on and sit on your own lap."

She kissed him again and took another chair. "Karel?"

"Yes. How did you know?"

"Albert called me. What goes there, Dad?"

"Filthy business, honey. The dirtiest, filthiest business I ever heard of." He picked up the telephone. "Give me Jim's Photo Shop, please. Jim? Doc Franchette. Could you take some flash shots of a face that has been beaten, catching all the bruises and discolorations? Unh hunh…filter? Well, take whatever equipment is necessary down to the Clinic and tell Albert I sent you. I want pictures taken from all angles to show every bruise she has. What? Oh, Karel Snowden. She's in One-Ten. She'll be sleeping and lights or flash won't waken her." He waited for a moment. "I'll tell you all about it, Jim, when I see you. In the meantime, keep it under your hat, will you? Thanks. Goodbye."

"How come?" asked Lisabeth.

"There's going to be a stink raised, and I want to be backed up to the hilt when it comes—and that reminds me of something else." He called the Clinic and asked to speak to his son.

"Albert, is Jenkins around?"

"Sure, Dad. Say, what's the matter with Karel? Happy said—"

"Never mind. I'll tell you later. Here's what I want you to do. Take Jenkins with you and examine Karel for criminal attack. I want all the physical findings, microscope analyses, everything. In other words, my fine doctor, give me all the dope you can possibly get on rape—pure and unadulterated rape."

He crashed the phone down in its cradle and turned to meet the shocked, questioning eyes of Lisabeth.

CHAPTER TWO

THAT NIGHT after supper Albert and his father sat in the latter's office. "You were right. There were all the signs, microscopic and all—and yet—"

The older man nodded. "Not enough damage to suit you, eh?"

"Frankly, there wasn't. Several other things, too. She had been beaten rather badly about the face, but there weren't any other physical signs of real damage. The hymen had been ruptured but there was almost no hemorrhage, indicating extreme care, which is something you don't find in criminal attack."

"We," said the Doctor with obvious satisfaction, "are not going to admit it, but here is the way it happened." He told Albert the whole story, including Jerry Booth's part.

"Now I see. That one point had me buffaloed for a while. It was there and yet it wasn't. What do you mean, we aren't admitting it?"

"We aren't admitting to Jerry Booth's role because we're going to show that that louse of a grandfather is the real culprit. He'll lay it on Jerry Booth and we'll make him try to prove it."

Albert grinned. "You're an old devil, Pop. I'm glad you love me."

"Don't let it swell your head. You toe the mark or I'll frame you, too."

The next morning Franchette was drinking his second cup of coffee when Maude ushered Sheriff Williams into the office. The little man got up. "Hi, Sam. How about a cup of coffee?"

Williams was ill at ease and showed it. "Well now, Miss Maude's coffee is got a rep. Guess I'll take a cup, please, ma'am."

Maude left the study and the Doctor lit a cheroot. "What's on your mind, Sam?"

Williams was a man who believed in getting things said quickly and succinctly, no matter the cost. "Doc, old Rathborne claims you kidnapped his granddaughter."

"Ummm, he does, does he? What do you know about that? Do I fill the bill as a picture of a kidnapper?"

"Hell, no," grumbled Williams, mauling his big black hat. "I told that old fool he was crazy but he kept on and threatened to call up the Governor and tell him I wasn't doin' my job. I thought I'd come 'round and talk to you about—Oh, thanks, Miss Maude. It sure smells good." He paused as he stirred in sugar.

"Well, Sam, the story is going to come out sooner or later, but I dread it because of what it'll do to the girl. She's in the Clinic now. You can easily prove that to yourself. I haven't kidnapped her. She came here of her own free will and accord because she didn't know where else to go. Now, here's the story."

The story left Williams, who had five daughters of his own, pale and grim. "I always knew there was something loose somewheres about him."

"Now, he's going to deny it, Sam, but we're loaded for him. We'll have pictures of her all beaten up and we'll have proof by Albert, Jenkins and myself that there was an attack. Naturally, he'll blame someone else, but I'd like to see him prove it."

Williams set the cup down. "Thanks for understandin', Doc. When a man puts pressure on the Sheriff, the Sheriff's gotta do something. I won't take no guff from the Rev no more."

"That's all right, Sam. Drop around any time."

As the Doctor finished his coffee, there came a pounding of hoofs, a creaking of harness and a mighty female voice profanely ordering her charges to halt, dammit, or be shot at sunrise. He bounded to his feet and went out to see a mountainous female climbing from a buckboard. It was Fannie Blumendahl.

"Greetings, you creaking, senile mockery of a man," she bellowed, beating the dust from her skirt and jodhpurs into which was crammed two hundred and ten pounds of belligerent woman.

"Come on in," he snapped testily, "and quit advertising my defalcations to the world at large."

Fannie went through the gate, snatching off a brilliant green kerchief to let the morning sun shine on her brassily golden hair, a color that Nature herself never meant to be on the head of a woman. Her plump face was jolly, full of good nature and fun, but her eyes were ice-hard, shrewd and calculating.

"Go to hell," she blared. "I'll see you in your grave, you tottering corpse. Got any bourbon in this house?"

"At this hour?" asked the Doctor, aghast.

"What the hell's wrong with the hour?" She shook his hand with a grip that made him wince. "So, as of old," she said, standing back and surveying him coldly, "you think you can get along without Fannie? Well, well, well. The older the man, the bigger the fool. That's what I always say."

"If that was all you always said, I could die happy," he sighed. "Come on in. I suppose you want to ruin some of Maude's excellent coffee with bourbon."

She followed him into the study, pulling dusty gauntlets from her hands and slapping her heavy thighs resoundingly with them. Franchette sneezed. "You always smell of horses and bring dust into the house," he said accusingly. "You, a woman with millions of dollars and yet riding around in an eighteen-ninety conveyance."

"I like it, so I do it. Maude!" she roared.

Maude entered, bearing a decanter of whiskey and a cup of hot, black coffee. "I heard you so I came prepared." Fannie hugged her while the little man watched them suspiciously.

"I find this visit of yours a little too well-timed to be coincidental."

"Who said it was coincidental?" retorted Fannie, lacing her coffee heavily with Brandsher's Special Age.

"You came to put me through the third degree," he said defensively, "so get along with it."

Her intense blue eyes sparkled at him over the cup. "A stooge tells me you have a problem in the form of a lovely, misunderstood, badly treated girl. Like all our problem girls, she's beautiful. Ain't it funny that all our problems are beautiful women? Looks like we'd draw a mud hen for a change."

"You're past the problem age," said the Doctor acidly. "You could qualify otherwise."

"You don't look so goddam hot either," she bit back, putting her cup down. "I'll have you know that in my day there wasn't a belle in the parish who could touch me. As for you, I doubt that you were ever any better than a bantam with aspirations to be a gamecock."

Maude cackled out loud and Dr. Franchette subsided, looking wounded. "Very well, I do have a problem, but I can handle it well enough alone."

"Certainly you can, Theodore, but why not tell me about it?" She was wheedling now and her voice went down to a stage whisper that rang through every room in the house.

He lifted his shoulders in a Gallic shrug. "Rathborne's daughter … er … granddaughter … terrible situation." He told her what had happened and during the telling her face underwent several changes in expression and color.

"Where is she now?" Her voice had a warm quality.

"At the Clinic. In that way I'll be able to keep her away from him. As you well know, Toni Salton had a shock similar to this— too similar for my ease of mind. There's no telling what a thing like this will do to Karel."

Fannie puffed and cracked the knuckles of her strong hands. "Damn! Double damn—that hateful old son-of-a-bitch. Bet you a dollar he's going to kick up some ruckus and get this boy in trouble just to save his own hide."

"His hide," spat the old man viciously, "is my own private property. I'll take it in my own way."

Fannie extracted an ivory holder from a shirt pocket that had been made especially for it and inserted a long Russian cigarette. When it was puffing to her satisfaction, she put the cup on the desk, leaned back and ejected a bank of blue smoke. "You can have him. I'll take care of the girl."

Dr. Franchette's beard fairly danced. "I seem to have no alternative," he sighed with pseudo-sorrow.

"Correct, and now that you realize it, I think I'll pay the child a visit. It takes me to do these things up right." She left soon afterward, her two red Morgans kicking up a cloud of saffron dust and throwing gravel all the way back to the porch.

The whole of her eccentric and independent person was expressed by the buckboard, her own trademark of defiance. As she clattered down the street, Dr. Albert Franchette looked out of his office window and chuckled. "Hey, Jenkins?"

"Yeah."

"Come here. I want you to see a character. She'll come barging in here in a minute, but first I want you to see her at a distance." He pointed to the street where Fannie was backing from her buckboard as it sagged and leaned precariously under her weight.

"What—who is she? I mean, why does she travel in that sort of rig?"

"Simply because she wants to. She lives in that tremendous pink stucco house up on the hill. She inherited it from her family. She's the last of a long line of thrifty and prosperous Fahenstocks and she's got more money than she can count. She fell hard for Isaac Blumendahl, a brilliant and industrious boy she met in college, and after years of determined pursuit, she finally won him in marriage. He had a flair for finance and investment and when he died, Fannie's already ample fortune was impregnable. Isaac also gave her a son, a brilliant chap who graduated from Johns Hopkins University with honors as a physician trained in psychiatry. She's now well past middle age but hale and hearty enough for a dozen people. She's the social empress for the community. What she says, goes. She spends her money freely, gives mammoth parties for the sole purpose of shocking her guests, is the anonymous—she thinks—donor to any worthy cause and runs the lives of as many people as she can. The town squirms under her iron fist, laughs at her idiosyncracies, forgives her and, above all, loves her."

Dr. Jenkins grinned and shook his head in amusement. "I'm looking forward to meeting her."

"You will very shortly. She's heard about Karel Snowden being here, I'll bet, and she smells another of Dad's cases where all sorts of fouled-up circumstances crop up. He and Fannie have unsnarled some Gordian knots that would curl your hair. He turns 'em up and she horns in. They bite at each other something fierce but they have a lot of affection and respect for each other. That's about all Dad does now—fish and nose out other folks' troubles."

"I subscribe to that regime wholeheartedly. I—"

The door flew open with a crash and Fannie stood on the threshold, glaring and beating dust from her jodhpurs with her long gloves.

"Dammit, you've seen me before," she roared. "Do I get the offer of a chair and a drink or do I go back and tell that old rake of a father of yours that you've let his Clinic go to hell?"

Albert pretended to be offended. "This is a place of peace, rest and quiet. I will not have all this noise and turmoil."

"Horse—!" she said and found herself a chair. "Ring for that little protegé of Theodore's—that little blonde hussy with the come-hither eyes—and tell her to bring the mixin's. I'm thirsty."

Dr. Jenkins doubled up in a fit of laughter and Fannie eyed him belligerently. "Who's the braying jackass?" she snapped. "Or are you ashamed of him?"

"Oh, excuse me … Mrs. Fannie Blumendahl … Dr. Jenkins."

"It's a pleasure, ma'am," said Jenkins, bowing low.

"How do you know it is?" she shot back.

Startled, he straightened up. "Er … I beg your pardon."

"I said, how do you know it's a pleasure? You haven't met me long enough to know. For all you know, I might turn out to be a hell-cat."

"I have a weakness for hell-cats," said Jenkins smoothly. "Especially those who travel about in buckboards."

Fannie looked at him keenly. "Humph!" She accepted a drink from Albert. "Tell me about this girl Theodore sent here."

Jenkins and Albert exchanged glances. "Well, she spent a quiet night and she seems all right now except for her fear that she'll have to go back to her grandfather."

Fannie's face was serious. "What can be done about that, Albert? After all, he *is* her legal guardian, and although Theodore wants to make a stir about it, think what it will mean to the child to have her life blighted like that."

"I think Dad means to prove criminal attack."

"But won't Rathborne claim the Booth boy did it?"

"He can claim it, but I doubt if he can prove it. The girl is filled with resentment, and she will swear that nothing happened between Jerry Booth and herself. *Something* happened, we know. I had Jenkins look at her, too."

Fannie compressed her lips. "Albert, what the hell is the world coming to? I agree with your father—I'd like to go after that treacherous old hypocrite with a gun." She shuddered and finished her drink. "What room is the kid in?"

"One-Ten. Try not to upset her, Fannie."

"That child needs some mothering. I'll upset her all right, but in the right way. There are some facets of medicine, son, that a woman with a kind heart and a broad, absorbent chest is better qualified to practice than you and all your degrees."

Albert smiled affectionately. "I'm sure you're right, Fannie. I know you'll do her good."

Fannie grunted and bounced to her feet. "I'll drop back on my way out and have another one. If you two are gone, I'll rustle for myself."

She strode down the hall with a solid step. Reaching room One-Ten, she opened the door without preliminaries. For a moment she and Karel stared at each other. Fannie felt a sweet, warm, choking sensation in her breast, a feeling she always had when she looked at an exceptionally beautiful girl who was young and in need of a helping hand.

"My dear, I'm Fannie Blumendahl. I've come to talk to you."

Karel nodded dully and inclined her head in the direction of the room's only chair.

Fannie sat inelegantly on her spine and spread her thick legs. "Karel, I'm a good friend of Dr. Franchette's."

The girl's expression brightened. "He's the kindest man in the world," she said in a low voice that was almost a sob.

"Theodore is a dear man," Fannie went on. "You are quite right to love him. He told me what happened."

Karel shrank back in her bed, her face white, making her soft hair seem darker as it spread in dishevelment on the pillow. "I'm not going back there," she said in a hoarse, rasping voice. "I'm not going back. I'll run away first. I'll become what he called me if I have to—but I'm not going back! I'm not going back—ever!" Her voice rose higher and her eyes became wide and fearful. "And if you're working with those welfare people who take other people where they don't want to go—"

Fannie stood up and walked over to the half-hysterical girl. "Shut up!" Her voice was like the crack of rifle fire and Karel caught her breath. For a moment the big woman stood there in frowning wrath until she saw that the girl had conquered her emotions. Then she smiled with such wholehearted vigor that a return smile twitched Karel's wan lips.

"Now then. That's better. I'm no ogre, honey, and I'm here to help, not to send you back to that old grandfather of yours. In fact, when Theodore Franchette and I put our heads together, we can do just about anything we set out to do. We say you'll never spend another night in that house."

It took Karel a while to digest the statement because fear had gnawed at her like a cancer since she had awakened that morning—sickening, weakening fear that people would disbelieve her and make her go back to him. Now that she had been told it never would be allowed to happen, she could hardly believe her own ears. Fannie sat on the side of the bed and placed a tremendous, jeweled hand over her slender one.

"That's right, honey. Let it soak in good. You won't have to go back. We'll see to it that you don't ever go back."

Karel looked with dazed wonder at the big, blonde woman. Then suddenly she seized the hand and carried it to her face, bowing her head over it. Hot tears poured from her eyes but she did not make a sound and Fannie gathered her to her capacious bosom. It was some time before Karel could speak and not once had she made a sound, a fact that Fannie found strangely upsetting. A body should yell and storm—that was the only way to cry—but Karel just dripped tears and seemed behind a wall of impenetrable silence.

The Reverend Rathborne was speaking to several of his most fanatical followers. "Brothers," he said sonorously, "this man has defiled my granddaughter. He has visited an abomination upon my house. This girl is the distillate of a thousand years of flawless, Anglo-Saxon breeding and he has treated her as a trollop. Brothers, God cries out for vengeance!" His eyes flitted over their sharp, intense faces and he felt reassured.

Two hours later Jerry Booth, seeing the bank of men plodding toward his rule cabin, was not pleased nor, on the other hand, was he particularly frightened. He felt discommoded.

"Hayseeds coming, Pop," he called to his father, who was putting a split white-oak bottom in a rocking chair that had seen its best days.

"What for?" asked his father, spitting a stream of tobacco through his fingers.

"Reverend Rathborne, I suppose. He must have found out."

"You oughta be more careful. You gonna *reely* git us run off one o' these days."

"I'll run and like it when the time comes," said Jerry calmly, "but right now I'm mostly mad."

When the group of fourteen men reached the frail picket fence, they paused for a moment and then, with true mob spirit, tore it down and walked over it. Jerry sat motionless on the rickety porch and eyed them. As they approached, he stood up.

"We don't want any," he announced crisply.

Obediah Dalton, a lanky, cadaverous man with deeply burning eyes like tiny forest fires in the distance, came to a halt as did his seven sons, four nephews and two brothers. Like Obediah, they were long of limb, thin of shank, with deep-sunk eyes that gleamed hungrily.

"Ye don't want whut?" demanded Obediah, clutching a long-barreled gun whose breechblock was the twist of a copper wire.

"Whatever you're selling, Slats," said Jerry insultingly.

"We ain't sellin' nuthin'," put in Luke, while Matthew, Mark and John nodded their shaggy heads.

"Then suppose you be making tracks."

"We," said Obediah, cocking his piece and bringing it up to the ready, "come to git you."

Wham! Obediah felt a stunning shock and his ancient piece seemed to disintegrate in his hands. His fingers felt around the nails.

Luke raised his gun slowly because he couldn't tell from where the shot had come and he was frightened. Again came the thunderous explosion of a large-caliber pistol and Luke's gun went the way of his Uncle's. It was then that Ed Booth chose to come from hiding, holding two nickled .45 Frontier model Colts low at his side.

"Room's gittin' sca'ce," he said softly. "Git!"

Then, so rapidly that the ear could scarcely distinguish the shots, the big Colts began to thunder. Guns fell apart in stiff, fearful hands and hats took sudden flight from shaggy, unwashed heads. The involuntary retreat from the blazing guns turned, in a matter of a split second, into a rout and soon Jerry and Ed Booth were alone, grinning at each other in swaggering triumph.

Obediah Dalton's retreat did not abate until he reached the sanctity of Sheriff Williams' office, sputtering with self-righteous indignation. Obediah, like many of his ilk, was perfectly willing to take the law into his own hands for his own ends, but when the fates turned on him, he immediately ran with his troubles to higher authorities. Complaining bitterly of his mistreatment at the hands of the Booths, he let the fact of his lynching bee out and in so doing implicated the Reverend Rathborne.

Three hours later Rathborne stood on his front porch and listened to what the Sheriff thought of a man of God inciting to riot.

"I don't know what your idea was, Preacher, but one more trick like that and I'll pop you in jail so fast you'll swear a miracle's come to earth."

"Sir," said Rathborne stiffly, "I resent your tone. I merely told the Daltons, who, as you know, are members of my congregation, that my home had been defiled. I did not suggest that they take any action. I might add that I at least got some action from them which I haven't as yet had from you."

"And you made a trip fifteen miles out in the sticks to complain. You picked the dumbest and orneriest bunch of nitwits in the whole parish to tell it to. Just a coincidence, of course."

"I don't like your tone of voice," repeated the other, a picture of outraged dignity.

"I don't give a damn if you don't," said Sheriff Williams bluntly. "I didn't come here to please you. I come to tell you what to expect if you ever try such a trick again. As for the Booths, they've pulled stakes. I went down there before I come here."

"My granddaughter is still at that Clinic. What do you propose to do about that?"

"I'm likely to take you to Jackson and put you in a padded cell if you come to me with any more of them silly tales about Dr. Franchette kidnappin' her. Made me feel a plumb damn fool goin' to the man's house askin' him how come he kidnapped your granddaughter. Doc says the gal's sick, and as far as I'm concerned, what he says goes." Then Williams' eyes narrowed. "Dr. Franchette told me there might somethin' else come of this deal and I'm waitin' to see what it'll be. I smell a dirty Indian in the brush heap."

Rathborne swayed and turned as pale as dough. "Get off my property," he hissed hoarsely.

"Hell, yes! It'll be a pleasure."

Dr. Franchette labored over a fly that he was tying. He boasted that he had a fly in every bush on every stream in Louisiana, and he was now trying to make up for some of the losses. "A Black Gnat," he complained to Maude, "is supposed to be black."

"So one would assume," she said placidly, her knitting needles flashing.

"Please do not be sarcastic. Lisabeth brought in some feathers the color of which baffles me. Nevertheless, I am certain they are not black."

"Dip them in ink," suggested Maude, yawning. He favored her with a sour glance and went back to tying his fly. A knock brought him stiffly upright.

"A dry bone knocking," he said with distaste. "A dry bone fastened to an arm bone, arm bone fastened to a shoulder bone—"

"Scapula and clavicle," corrected Maude gently.

"It's a song," he explained. "The point is, the only man I know who knocks with dry bones is our good Rathborne."

"Then answer the door. I certainly don't want to see him."

Sighing gustily, the spry little man put down his fly and walked to the front door.

"What do you want?" he asked belligerently.

"I have come to ask when you propose to release my granddaughter."

"I don't see how that could possibly concern you," snapped Franchette. "She's never going to put foot in your house again."

For a moment the Reverend Rathborne was incapable of speech. "Do you mean to stand there and tell me that you are going to try to take my own flesh and blood away from me?"

"I mean to stand here and tell you that very thing," said the other.

"Theodore, have you gone mad?"

"Hardly. However, you might consider *yourself* in that light, attacking your own blood like a savage gone amuck."

Compressing his lips into a tight line, Rathborne looked at the Doctor in silence for a moment. "I don't think you know what you're doing."

"I am quite well aware of what I'm doing. You will find that out very shortly, I'm thinking."

"I shall go at once to that abattoir you call a Clinic and demand that she be allowed to leave in my custody."

"And," said Franchette cheerfully, "if you do, Albert shall be pleased to throw you out on your ear."

"I shall then take recourse to the law."

"I think that would be better. It would bring things to a head quicker."

Rathborne turned abruptly on his heel and walked off the porch, stumbling on the top step and catching himself on all fours on the brick walk. Dr. Franchette chuckled nastily. "I never have any luck. I was hoping you'd break your damn neck." With a malevolent glance, the Minister picked himself up and walked stiffly away.

Two hours later Franchette got a phone call. "Hello, Theodore? This is Aaron Marvin. Would you mind coming up here to the Courthouse. Reverend Rathborne is here making all sorts of wild charges. I can't make heads or tails of any of it."

"Sure, Aaron. I'll be there in a few minutes." He hung up and grinned at Maude. "Rathborne went to Judge Marvin. This is just what I wanted." He picked up the phone again and called the Clerk of Court. "Simm … Dr. Franchette. Say, Simm, will you take your seal and dash over to the Clinic and take some depositions for me? Good. See Albert and Jenkins. They'll explain it all to you. I don't have time. Bring the depositions to the Judge's chambers when you're through."

Rathborne sat in haughty disdain while Theodore grinned satanically at him.

The Judge, portly and bald, built a judicious tent of his fingers and said, "Now, Reverend, what is this all about?"

"I shall repeat myself," said Rathborne. "This man is keeping my granddaughter away from me by saying that she is ill. Moreover, he says she'll never come back to me. I desire some sort of order from this Court remanding her to my custody immediately."

Judge Marvin looked at the Doctor. "What's this all about, Theodore?"

Franchette grinned again. "I say she's ill. My son and his colleague will concur. Furthermore, she does *not want* to live with this old goat here."

Rathborne made a furious noise and the Judge palmed a smile. "But surely you must know that you can't keep his ward from him simply because she doesn't like him. He's her legal guardian."

"Her reasons, which we shall examine right now, prove that she has good and sufficient cause for her attitude. Patience, Aaron. Some depositions will be here shortly."

Rathborne leaped to his feet, his face livid. "If you persist in this fiction that you started yesterday, I will sue you to the limit of the law. She was practically caught in an assignation with that Booth person and she has fabricated this fabric of pure lies."

The door opened and Simm Evarts came in with a handful of documents. He glanced at Rathborne, his fat face as hard as iron. "There ain't been a lynching in this parish in forty years," he said as though he were strangling. Rathborne reeled and sat down, his long fingers plucking at his vest buttons.

"It's a monstrous lie—a lie I tell you!" he shrieked.

"Be quiet," said the Judge ominously. "Let me see the papers, Simm."

"You have there," said Evarts, his voice squeaking angrily out of control, "two statements. One each by the doctors and—ah, hell, you read 'em."

Judge Marvin adjusted his glasses and read rapidly. His face went pale and then purple. Finally he rose slowly to his feet. "I have heard of these things but ... Well, maybe we had better go at this differently. Rathborne, I have here sworn depositions from two doctors whom we respect highly—"

"With whom I agree thoroughly," said Franchette. "I, too, examined her." The lie fell shamelessly from his lips. Judge Marvin, his face still turkey-red, nodded and went on. "These doctors say that the girl has been criminally attacked. She showed, upon admission, signs of a bad beating. There..." He cleared his throat angrily, "...were other signs which we need not go into here. The girl in a sworn statement says you called her filthy names, forced her to disrobe in your presence and then attacked her. She states that later she ran over to Dr. Franchette's house for protection. Now, sir, what have you to say for yourself?"

Rathborne, having regained some of his composure, rose to his feet. "I have just heard the most monstrous lie of my life. The girl is evil like her mother. I almost caught her in the act with the Booth boy. That I beat her I will not deny. A man must follow the voice of God when dealing with his own blood in matters of discipline."

"The thing is, Rathborne," rapped out Dr. Franchette. "You *say* you *almost* caught her in the act with Booth. Can you prove it?"

"Of course not. How can I? I didn't actually see them with my own eyes."

"I think," put in the little man, "that we could prove you did it. We can prove that it was done, we can prove that you beat her—on your own admission—and we have her sworn testimony that you did. What sort of a chance do you think you'd have with a jury, Rathborne?"

The Minister tottered and sat heavily. "This is more than the soul can bear," he said hollowly.

Judge Marvin sat eyeing the cadaverous man, so choked with fury that he could not speak. Finally he turned to Franchette. "Will you prefer charges, Theodore?"

"It would appear that this is a matter for the District Attorney—a crime against society. However, as far as I am personally concerned, I would prefer to let matters lie unless Rathborne chooses to carry them further."

Judge Marvin rose to his feet. "I'd like to speak to you alone a moment, Theodore."

In another room the Judge frowned heavily. "Confidentially, of course, the Grand Jury would have to find a true bill. That would present difficulties. Just between you and me, I don't think we could get a conviction on the evidence."

"Of course we couldn't," said the Doctor, grinning. "We have scared him out of his wits though, and that's enough for me. I will wait for a while and have him turn the girl's guardianship over to me or Fannie Blumendahl as a price for our silence. I think it will work."

"I think so, too, and I must admit that the legal aspect is hardly favorable. Ministers carry a certain implied respect and actually what we have is her word against his."

Dr. Franchette lit a cheroot and smiled. "Let it go. I don't think we'll have any trouble with him. How did you manage to swallow the thing as easily as you did? I thought I'd have a job of convincing on my hands."

Judge Marvin massaged his jaw. "Never liked that fellow somehow. Something about him doesn't ring true and never has."

When they returned to the outer office, Rathborne was still deathly pale. His lips were blue and his cheeks gray. Dr. Franchette eyed him carefully. Heart, he thought. Maybe he won't be with us long.

"It has been decided, Rathborne," said the Judge, "that action be deferred until your own actions dictate the necessity for reopening the matter. If I were you, I'd let the Doctor have his way because that appears to me to be your only salvation. I need not tell you what would happen if this matter should become public knowledge. I doubt that your congregation would like it very much."

Rathborne shuddered, seeming to share the opinion.

He turned a stricken face to Dr. Franchette. "What do you want me to do?"

"I want you to go home and hold your peace. Later you will be contacted and instructed."

Rathborne pulled himself to his feet and tottered from the room. At this point Jim Barnes came in.

"Albert said you'd be here, Doc. I got the prints."

"Good. Send me the bill. Here, Aaron, I want you to see these."

The prints were garishly clear and showed each bruise vividly. One eye was dark-ringed and swollen half-closed. She seemed defenseless and lost as she lay in innocent sleep, her luxuriant hair in tumbled disarray on the white pillow. Even the roomy hospital gown could not conceal the lovely, ripe lines of her young body. The Judge swore softly and handed the prints back.

"Whatever you do, Theodore, I'm for it one hundred per cent." Then, musingly, "What do you suppose is going to happen to her? What does happen to girls like this?" He shook his head. "I'll tell you one thing—this isn't the last time by a long shot that some panting he-man is going to try to get his hot hands on her."

CHAPTER THREE

PHILLIP RICHARD GAMBLE arrived in Kenton without fanfare or advance notice. He drove his modest coupe up to the Ford Agency and asked Jeff Peters for a job.

Jeff, almost as wide as he was tall, sat in a squeaky swivel chair with his hands folded over his rotund stomach.

"What can you do?"

"Anything. Keep books, run the front. In a pinch, wash and grease."

"Ummm. You sound like a boy with some sense. Where did you get it?"

"I'm a forester by education."

"Forester? What the hell do you want a job here for if you got that much education?"

Gamble shut his jaws tight and pushed back an unruly lock of hair. "Let's say I don't like forestry."

"Okay, you said it. Now, how come you want a job here?"

"I don't have to have a job, Mr. Peters. Not here at any rate. I'm sorry I bothered you."

"No bother, son. I'm just a meddlesome old man. No more questions. I'll give you a try. We'll see how it works out. When can you start?"

"Tomorrow."

"See you at nine in the morning. Pay is fifty a week."

"Fair enough." Gamble pulled a discolored straw hat over his straight blond hair and walked briskly out of the building. As he walked through the door, he collided with a girl. Mumbling an apology and without even bothering to look at her, he walked to his car.

The girl was a beautiful brunette whose body struggled between classic slimness and luxuriant voluptuousness, the result being one to stir the pulses and send blood pressures soaring. Annette Peters was well aware of the effect of her body and flaunted her invitations with just the necessary touch of good taste to avoid seeming brazen. No one would have called her forward, yet there was always an unspoken "but" behind any description of her.

Her full, damp lips pouted somewhat as she walked into her father's office and sat on the edge of his desk. "Who was that handsome thing going out as I came in?"

Jeff Peters grunted and glanced at his daughter. "Young 'un. Come in lookin' for a job."

"What's his name?"

"Plumb fergot to ask 'im."

"Did you give him the job?"

"Sure. Needed a bookkeeper. Said I'd give him a try at it, anyway. How come you're so interested?"

"Because he's handsome and there aren't many handsome men in town."

"Never noticed."

"You wouldn't. He's tall, has good shoulders and holds himself well. His hair is red-blond and his teeth are good, what I saw of them. He's got deep, thoughtful eyes and real curly lashes."

"What about his nose?"

"Thin, patrician, but not indicating coldness."

"How does he like his steaks cooked?"

"Rare. He loves good things to eat. I can tell from his mouth. Bet he could kiss good, too."

Peters chuckled deep down in his capacious paunch. "Now if I was the Sheriff and this lad was a bank robber, I'd have him pegged before he could turn around—'cept unless he could maybe get some doctor to do plastered surgery on him."

"Plastic," she corrected.

"Hunh?"

"Never mind—I give up. When does he start to work?"

"Tomorrow."

"Good. I'll be here."

"Thought so. Poor feller ain't got a chance. Specially when Janey Hardwicke seen 'im too. Saw her standin' across the street just before he come in."

Annette uttered a very unladylike noise. "She had better stay away from here. This is strictly my preserve from now on."

Jeff, who dearly loved to badger his daughter, said, "Well, you can't never tell. I remember that Edwards boy you brought back from the University that time when—" The crash of his office door made him wince. He had replaced the glass only a week before when she had left in a rage, slamming the door with such force that his desk had been covered with a thick coating of glass fragments.

Dick Gamble was a young man of many tastes, goals, opinions and imaginings. His idyllic childhood had little prepared him for the world and its many ways, and the death of his adoring parents when he was seventeen had launched him into early manhood like a ship without a rudder. Since nothing had ever really touched him, he knew how to cope with nothing. He floundered helplessly, unable to make decisions and always trodding the paths of least resistance. Girls took up more and more of his time until at last he was struck full in the face by the fact that he wouldn't graduate with his class. Shocked—and tongue-lashed by the fury of the aunt who had taken him in—he lied about his age, joined the Navy and wound up in the Pacific jungles fighting the Japs. After three exhausting years, he had returned to the States with a case of chronic cynicism stretched smotheringly over his inner uncertainties. He was examined for and received his high school diploma and spent four years at the University, where he juggled his course four times and graduated as a forestry major. He seemed now to hate the woods, but actually he did not. He could not stand their staunch sense of solid endurance which, to his restlessly seeking mind, was almost an insult. Had he been less sensitive, he would not have gone to such lengths in professing his hatred but would have simply dropped the matter. And, without doubt, he hid from himself the fact that he had taken forestry in school only because he had no other sense of direction.

Dick stowed his clothes away in the dismal closet in the room he had rented from Mrs. Pinkney and sat for a while on the huge four-poster bed. The place depressed him, a feeling he could have better done without since he was in continual battle with his moody spirits. He had a job, he had a car and he had a place to lay his head. That should be enough for the time being, he told himself. He dressed in khaki shorts and T shirt and left the stuffy little room. On the verandah Mrs. Pinkney sat rocking monotonously, her fat hands folded placidly in her lap.

"Oh, Mr. Gamble. I didn't know it was you."

"Yes'm," he answered politely. "Is there any place where a man might swim?"

"Of course, the pool—No, I guess not there either. It's private and you'd have to have an invitation. The members don't hand them out very freely either—I can tell you that."

"I'd prefer a stream anyway," he said.

"Oh, yes. Well, there are several. Petit Paul, that's nearest. You go down the road—the road west till it crosses the highway, and just below the bridge should be a place." Dick thanked her, walked down the flagged path and got in his car.

In the South women do not tag after men—obviously, that is, and as he drove away from Mrs. Pinkney's, two sharp eyes followed him, lost him while their owner dashed to a blue convertible and then caught up as the sleek little car was gunned unmercifully and regained lost ground. From then on it proceeded behind him at a decorous pace until at last he pulled up beside the bridge and stopped. The blue car shot forward and was soon lost in the distance.

Dick walked into the cool stillness of the hardwood forest bordering the tiny creek, resenting its cool aloofness, and was soon lost to sight. Five minutes after he disappeared, the blue coupe slid noiselessly over the crest of the hill and crept down to the bridge, stopping with the faintest whisper of a brake squeal.

A girl got out, clad in skin-tight white shorts and light green jersey. She was rather tall, her legs long and golden tan, her waist slim and pointed breasts erect. They staggered slightly as she walked, suggesting that they were without restraint. Their sharp tips wove delightful little geometric figures on the loose jersey as she walked down the embankment. She, too, was soon swallowed up in the woods.

Dick floundered noisily and comfortably in the biting chill of the clear water, naked, as he loved to swim. He felt gloriously free of the pressures that had been on him for months. Laughter bubbled up as he flung himself bodily from the water to rest on a log half submerged in midstream. Depression in youth is rarely rooted deeply, and though Dick was twenty-seven, his disorganized past had slowed his maturity at an age when many men are doddering and staggering beneath the load of wife and children, having lost their snap and elasticity in the mad scramble for sustenance and security. Suddenly he caught his breath, sat perfectly still for a fleeting second and then, with a smothered exclamation, he slid off the log with precipitous haste. In water up to his armpits and feeling relatively safe, he frowned at the bank above him where the girl stood laughing musically.

"That," he said bitingly, "was a low Irish trick."

"Scandinavian and French," she said, her teeth showing white and clean. "I'm Janey Hardwicke, your next-door neighbor."

"Hardwicke isn't French or Scandinavian."

"Names can be changed. You're Dick Gamble and you're going to work at the Ford place—at least you applied and almost ran over my deadliest enemy."

"You seem to know a lot about me. Everything practically, now that you've seen me naked. How long were you standing there?"

"Long enough to …" She stopped and turned pink.

"Go ahead," he said maliciously. "Why not tell me everything you saw?"

She extracted a cigarette from a small bag held to her wrist by a thong and lit it, obviously stalling to cover her perturbation. "I saw enough," she said evasively, blowing a cloud of smoke in his direction.

"You did?" he asked. "Then it's my turn—come on in."

"Like this?" She looked at her expensive sports clothes, her arms out wide.

"Of course not. Like I am."

Her eyes narrowed as she watched him silently for a few seconds. "You say what you think, don't you?"

"I think maybe we are both pretty lucky," he retorted. "Why, I haven't been caught like this in at least a month."

"Now you're trying to make me sore." She sat down, the legs of her shorts allowing a slight shred of flesh-tinted nylon to show. Dick's pulses hammered heavily and, in his cynicism, he took the attitude of, what have I got to lose. "I hope you have a strong constitution."

"Why?"

"Because you're sitting not ten feet from my clothes and I intend to get into them."

Her breath caught momentarily in her throat and her muscles tensed but she smiled at him gracefully. "Come ahead. I don't run easily."

"You'd run like a rabbit and you know it," he challenged.

"Try me."

He shrugged. "Maybe you won't run from the sight of me because you've already seen me, but I could make you take off like a ruptured gooney for other reasons."

Her laugh was musical and free. "Try me."

"I will." With a strong stroke he crossed the deep part of the pool, and with a magnificent leap he caught a low-hanging limb and climbed it hand-over-hand until he was over the bank. Then he let go and dropped at her feet. He stood there for a moment, his virile manliness openly daring her to run. She paled but didn't move. Studying her, he walked casually over to his clothes and put them on.

He returned and sat beside her as she reclined in the leaves, her heart thumping madly. The sight of him pulling out of the water, his redly bronzed hide rippling with long, finely conditioned muscles had struck her like a sharp, thin prod.

Her facial expression, however, revealed nothing of her inner turmoil or her realization that another test might be coming up which she did not know how to handle. She had pride but also a strong desire to place him once and forever out of the reach of Annette Peters. Janey was certainly no stranger to love but even in her forthright existence, the situation in which she now found herself was unparalleled in its sudden crisis.

His eyes laughed at her. "You're doing pretty good—so far."

"So far?" Her voice was not quite as steady as she wished.

"That's what I said—so far."

"What comes next?"

"What do you think?"

"I know what you must be thinking."

"What?"

"That I'm a bitch to come out here like this and watch you swim."

He shrugged carelessly. "Maybe you have a hunger for a man like I have for … well, for a woman like you."

She sat up, a frown marring the smooth expanse of her brow. "You make it sound so ... so evil and mechanical. In fact, I don't think I'm going to like you at all."

Dick's eyes narrowed. This was the sort of female that he did not like—the sort who liked to play and then to pretend that she had not played after all.

"This," he said with a tight look hardening his face, "will probably be something new in your life, but it is entirely possible that I won't like you either. You just finished pegging yourself rather neatly, I think."

Suddenly she moved close to him, her breath fanning his cheek. The action was almost one of apology, and one pointed breast thrust itself insistently against his arm. Turning to her, he smiled inwardly, first at her overwhelming vanity and then at his own unbridled opportunism. Their lips together, he pushed her gently back to the ground. She arched her long body up to him and he deftly removed the white shorts. Then, his weight coming down hard against her, it seemed that a skein of magic madness closed over her face, and a quake of rapture shook through her body.

Janey was, in her own way, experienced, but in all of her affairs she had kept the upper hand by a subtlety that led her object on while she kept her own head and observed, as it were, from a distance, until she knew that she had the situation under complete control. Dick, in one swift moment, had used her own technique against her, and when a draft of cool air struck her, she returned to consciousness with a snap that hurt. She was panicked to find herself at his mercy, utterly bereft of her self control. With a gasp that was at the same time a cry, she tore herself free of his embrace, leaped to her feet and raced blindly through the woods toward her car.

Dick shrugged, grinned and looked at the expensive shorts he held in his hand. Then he, too, jumped up and ran after her, calling to her to stop. Janey heard his voice but it only added to her panic and she ran all the faster. Suddenly bursting out of the woods, she realized in one blood-freezing moment that beside her car there was another and that she was clad only in brief, filmy panties and halter. Her hand went to her mouth and she came to a stop. Instantly recognizing that the occupant of the other car was Annette Peters, she was confronted with what amounted to catastrophe. While she stood there on the narrow pit bank, stricken with horrified indecision, Annette climbed with leisurely grace from her car and stood on the macadam, a wicked grin on her face.

"If I just had a camera now—"

Dick burst from the woods, waving the shorts, "Hey, you ran off without these. And you ran just as I predicted." He saw Annette standing on the road, and her grin was as plain as a neon sign on a dark night. "Oh—oh," he breathed as he came to a stop.

Janey, finally breaking the bonds that held her, ran down in the dry ditch and up on the shoulder of the road.

"Uh ... don't you want your shorts?" he called uncertainly.

"She's practicing up for some cult thing that makes its initiates go naked from the chest down," said Annette maliciously. "Funny thing, too. I shouldn't have thought that she needed practice."

With a sob of rage and chagrin, Janey climbed in her car and flogged the motor mercilessly as she left the vicinity with all possible speed, leaving Dick ruefully holding the shorts at half mast. With a baffled sigh, he dropped them in the grass and climbed to the edge of the road where Annette waited for him.

"Must have been fun," she said.

Dick took a quick glance at her and what he saw attracted him as much as had Janey, but her attitude toward the other girl's unfortunate position annoyed him.

"How would you know?" he asked bluntly.

"I've been told."

"You sound like the voice of experience itself."

A tiny frown appeared on her forehead. "I don't like your tone."

He shrugged. "Your pardon, I'm sure. I've been in town seven hours and already two beautiful women are tilting for my charms. I'm overwhelmed."

"What makes you think we're tilting for your charms?" she flared hotly.

"I can't speak for you," he said insolently, "but the departed sister certainly had designs. She, however, was a sissy and a fraud like most forward girls and when the chips are down—"

"You mean, when the shorts are off."

He nodded. "Have it your way. In any event, she couldn't take it."

"You *are* horrible," she breathed, shocked.

"Oh, Jesus. You're another one, I suppose. I was hoping for better stuff in Kenton."

Annette who was, like Janey, no better than she should be, was appalled at his blunt speech. "I think," she said choking a little, "that you'd better know who I am."

"You think that might make a difference?"

"It had better."

"Well then, do tell. I'm already impressed. Just who are you, chick?"

She gasped and clenched her hands. "I'm Annette Peters, that's who, and you'd better watch your manners."

He shrugged. "And in what way is Annette Peters any better than Richard Gamble?"

"I am the daughter of the man you go to work for tomorrow—*if* you go to work."

Dick swallowed but maintained a straight face. "I thought he was hiring me as a bookkeeper. I didn't know it included being an off-hour gigolo. I think I'll resign if it does. There are some things at which I balk."

"I can hardly believe it," she retorted sarcastically, with a pointed look at Janey's shorts lying in the grass.

He threw back his head and laughed. "Too bad she took them off for nothing, isn't it? She's probably kicking herself already— that's how it is with these no-at-the-last-minute bitches. Always sorry when it's too late. If you see her, give her my condolences."

CHAPTER FOUR

FANNIE BLUMENDAHL crossed her thick legs and gazed through the amber depths of her highball. "Well, Theodore, now that we have the girl, what do we do next? She's supposed to graduate in two weeks but it appears that she won't, according to Abel Sumner. He say's she's brilliant but hasn't been applying herself."

Dr. Franchette put his drink on his old roll-top desk and fumbled for cheroot and matches until he had a smoke going. "If you want my candid opinion, the sort of stuff that Abel Sumner and his fellow idiots grind out is pretty sterile grist for young minds. No wonder she doesn't apply herself. No one but the dull and prosaic ever apply themselves to such emasculated tripe."

Fannie nodded emphatically. "I'm glad you said that. As far as I can see, it doesn't matter a damn whether she has that kind of an education or not. I have every intention of marrying her off to some personable man who will appreciate her innate value and who won't mind if she can't recite Virgil or recall the date and details of the Diet of Worms."

Franchette pulled thirstily at his drink and put it down again. "As for where she'll stay, I've been wanting to talk to you about that. She's ready to leave the Clinic now. I talked to Albert this morning. He says she's been there too long now. The atmosphere isn't too hot for a well person."

"Does he consider her well?"

The Doctor shrugged. "Physically, of course she is. I never was bothered about that. My concern is for the psychic trauma she might have suffered."

"Never mind your big words," Fannie blared noisily. "What do they mean?"

"And you with a psychiatrist for a son?"

She sighed. "I wish to hell he'd come on home. He and Toni seem to be doing the Pacific playgrounds from Tonga to Tahiti."

"I wish he was here, too. He did a good job on Toni even if he did get his transference mixed and was sucked into a counter-transference. We may need him."

"Those words!" she protested indignantly. "What do they mean?"

"Oh, they are simple terms meaning psychic damage. If you mash a finger, you have trauma. If you get a black eye, you suffer trauma. If your father beat you every day for breakfast when you were young, you'd probably suffer trauma in several ways."

"I came to discuss her eventual home," she said, dropping her interest in terms. "You seem pretty calm about it so I can only take that to mean that you will offer no objection to my taking her."

"I was hoping you'd offer," he replied. "I fish a lot and Maude is as quiet as a scared man in a cemetery. Karel would do all right here, but I would rather see her with you. Your parties would give her a better social atmosphere."

Fannie snorted. "Are you kiddin'? Those brawls are for my own gratification at seeing one and all lick my boots because they think I'm the Dowager Empress. I doubt that I'll let her attend, even." She stuck a cigarette in her ivory holder, lit it and canted it rakishly in her mouth. "Thanks, anyway, you creaking old bag of bones. I think you're paying me as much of a compliment as you could, what with your professional jealousy and all."

"Who's jealous?" he wanted to know. "I let you into this against my better judgment in the first place."

"Nuts," she said. "You couldn't have done without me. What do we have to fear from Rathborne?"

"Nothing. He's subdued completely."

"Well, whenever he gets around to handing over her custody to me legally, let me know. I'll go by on my way out and pick her up. I wonder if there's anything at her home she'll want."

"Clothes, maybe, although he never gave her much in the way of fine feathers. Only her own flair for projecting something of her own personality into her clothes saved her from being dowdy."

"I'll see that she has 'em," said Fannie grimly. "The very finest and all she wants."

"That's right, go on and spoil her."

"I have every intention of spoiling her." She sobered for a moment. "Think of it, Theodore. I'll have a daughter. I've always wanted one." He looked at her steadily but refrained from speaking. For once he could see deeply within the woman and what he saw made him remain quiet.

Half an hour later Fannie walked with heavy heels into the Clinic and burst into the twin offices. Dr. Jenkins, clad only in shorts and shirt, was tying his tie before a tall mirror. He gave a startled exclamation and darted into the little washroom. Fannie exploded into a roar of laughter that made the walls resound. Albert came through another door, taking off his hat. "What's all the noisy joy about?"

"Jenkins," said Fannie, still shaking with mirth. "He forgot to lock the door and I caught him in his drawers. Glad you dropped in. I'm taking Karel home with me."

Albert looked at her closely. "That's really fine of you, Fannie. I think you'll make a wonderful mother for her."

"Oh ..." Fannie blushed furiously. "I'll do what I can," she said, looking out of the window. "What did she bring with her?"

"Nothing but what she had on."

"Good. I'll let you know as soon as I can how she fares under a new regime."

"It's too soon yet," said Albert, shedding his coat and tie, "and she's still very depressed. She's young though and maybe she'll snap right out of it. Maybe just a sense of freedom amid peaceful surroundings will do it. It isn't nice, Fannie, to live in a state of perpetual fear."

"I know," she growled. "I'll break the neck of anyone who brings fear around my house or so much as—" The door slammed and Dr. Jenkins came from the washroom with a look of stern reproof on his face.

"Do you generally go bursting into rooms without knocking?"

"Old habit of mine," replied Fannie, wheezing with laughter. "Jesus, those legs of yours, all hairy and—"

"Spare me," said Jenkins, turning pink and holding up a palm. "Deride me not before my colleague."

"To hell with you and your college or colleague or whatever you said. I got things to do … g'bye." The door banged as she left and Jenkins winced. "Why is she always so noisy?"

"That, son, is Fannie Blumendahl. You learn to expect it. Instead of annoying the patients, they start grinning and seem to feel better. Christmas she came with her buckboard full of champagne and got half the staff tight. We almost had to get some citizens to come in and take over. She threatened to withhold a stiff donation if we fired any of the girls. The donation came through, by the way. That's why you and the new wing arrived simultaneously."

"A marvelously acute woman," said Jenkins piously. "How do you suppose she knew you'd select me?" His colleague made a very disrespectful sound with his mouth.

When Fannie got to room One-Ten, Karel was already dressed, looking rather wan and fearful.

Fannie grinned at her. "Honey you're going home with me.

The girl's great eyes grew round and her chin trembled a little. "With you, Mrs. Blumendahl? Home? *Home!*" She seemed to taste the word over and over. She averted her eyes and her chin sank slowly to her breast. A moment later she wept for the second time with quiet intensity on the broad, comfortable breast of the big woman who was so loud, so bluff and yet so kindly, who dressed abominably and who always seemed to smell of horses.

"All right," Fannie rumbled. "That's enough for now. Later you can beller all over the place. The thing to do now is to get out of here. First thing you know you'll be sick, sure enough. Now, honey, is there anything at your house you want to get?"

"Yes, there are..." Her head went up and she shuddered. "No... no... *no*."

"*Yes!*" The voice had the crisp lash of a whip. "Whatever you want, we'll go get it. You don't even have to come in. You can wait in the trap and I'll get whatever you want."

"I want the picture of my mother," she said in a small, weary voice. "It's in the bottom of my trunk."

"You'll have it. Anything else?"

"N-no."

"What about clothes?"

She raised her eyes again. "Yes, of course—clothes." Her voice had no animation. It seemed dull and lifeless and she glanced self-consciously at the cheap cotton dress she wore. Fannie saw the glance, heard the lack of enthusiasm in her voice.

"On second thought," Fannie said. "We'll leave the damn things there. What you need is a whole new wardrobe and, by God, you shall have it, from soup to nuts."

Karel shook her head dazedly. Things were happening too fast for her comprehension. Far from the sickening fear of having to go back to her grandfather, here was a rich woman who spoke easily of taking her home, of buying her new clothes. With her mind still blank, Karel followed her out to the buckboard and looked with admiration at the fine Morgan horses who stood restively, shining like red bronze statues in the bright sun. "Ohh-h-h, Mrs. Blumendahl. They're lovely."

"Thanks. If you can appreciate good horseflesh, then you're a bit of all right. Get in and we'll get going."

Fannie roared at the horses and they immediately swung around in answer to the rein and started off at a smart trot. She pulled them to a halt in front of the parsonage and climbed out with her usual ungainly grace.

"What room, honey?"

"Through the hall, and just before you get to the dining room, you turn left. It's the second door from the living room."

"Okay. Stay put till I get back."

Fannie was about to open the door when Rathborne opened it from the inside.

"What can I do for you?" he asked in chilled accents.

"Not a goddamned thing except get out of my way," said Fannie. "I came to get some of your granddaughter's possessions."

"Madame, I forbid you to enter this house."

Fannie slid a short-handled whip from her wrist where it was secured by a thong. She reversed it and smacked the heavy handle in the palm of her gloved hand. "How would you like to have me part that brush for you, you rake-handled tub-thumper?"

"I shall have to remind you," he said, retreating a step, "that this is my house. My granddaughter is an ingrate and deserves nothing of what I have given her. What she has, she received from my bounty and has now forfeited all her right to it."

"She wants nothing but a picture," snarled Fannie. "I wouldn't let her wear a single damn rag you ever bought her. In fact, I'd fire any servant I have if I ever caught her with such shoddy clothes on, so you can stand aside, brother, because I'm coming in." She barged ahead and the Reverend Rathborne stepped quickly aside.

"If that is all she wants," he began, but Fannie was already far down the hall. With a jerk she threw up the trunk lid, pawed through a few clothes and came up with a faded photograph wrapped in cellophane and carefully tied with a blue ribbon. She thrust it into her bosom and walked back to the porch. As she suspected, Rathborne was halfway to the buckboard, where the girl sat tight and stiff with fear, her wide eyes watching him in stricken fascination. Fannie's whip uncoiled like a striking snake and exploded with a sharp report.

He started and spun around. "Just stay the hell away from that trap," she barked, "or I'll cut you to ribbons and I'd love the chance."

"I have a few words to say to my granddaughter," he said stiffly.

"Say it on your death bed," advised Fannie, smacking the handle of the whip into her palm suggestively. "Maybe she'll listen to you then, although I shall advise against it."

Rathborne's deep-set eyes were hellish. "Madam, I wish to say to you that you will one day be sorry for your part in this. You and that doctor, too. You have my most solemn word for it."

"Sir," mimicked Fannie, "I wish to say to you that there is a right smart chance that in your effort to see that we are sorry, you could easily get your tail in a crack. I can guarantee it."

"It seems to mean nothing to you and Franchette that you rob me of my kin."

"I thought you said she didn't deserve your bounty—whatever that is."

"The Master forgave," he declared sententiously. "I could hardly do less."

"That's what you say, but to date your record does not speak in your favor. By one single act, Rathborne, you have shown yourself unfit to be the guardian of a young girl. You may thank Franchette's tolerance that you are not now sitting in jail. Now get the hell out of my way before I beat your brains out." Rathborne stepped nimbly from her path and watched her with steady, burning eyes as she chirruped to her horses and drove out of sight.

"Mrs. Blumendahl—"

"Got enough of that Mrs. Blumendahl stuff, honey. Call me Fannie."

Karel looked at her for a long time and then said in a small voice, "I wish you were my mother."

Fannie stiffened as a hot, choking mass rammed itself into the region of her larynx. The landscape swam wetly and she dabbed furiously at her eyes with a huge bandanna handkerchief.

"After that, honey, you could call me Puddintain and I wouldn't raise my voice. If you ever want to call me mother, I'd be proud to have you do it."

Karel, whose spirit had been somewhat tethered as a safety precaution, now leaned back in her seat and let a trickle of free laughter flow from her throat.

"What's funny?" asked Fannie.

"I wasn't laughing at you. I just feel happy. It's a strange, wonderful feeling."

Fannie glanced at her curiously. "Honey, how old are you?"

"I'm eighteen. I'll be nineteen in September. Why?"

"I was just wondering. You have a grown-up way of speaking. I notice that words come easily to your lips."

"They should," she said bitterly. "I've lived in a puddle of words, words, words ever since I came to Kenton. I read because I could play with no one and I had to listen to Grandfather. He talks endlessly. He never stops."

Fannie patted her hand. "That's all over now. From now on you'll live as normal a life as I can make for you, although living with me will probably bore you to tears."

"I don't think so," Karel said candidly. "I think just being with you will make me very happy."

"You can't be happy all the time any more than you can subsist on a diet of mushrooms. There'll be ups and downs, glad and sad moments. You and I might even have spats."

"I've been down so long that I think I can stay up a long time and please, Mrs. Blumendahl, don't let's ever have spats. I don't want to oppose you in anything."

"Who'n hell ever gave you that idea?" flared Fannie. "You oppose me in anything you want to. If I can't make you understand what I try to put over, then you bite back. I don't want any spineless 'yes' gal around me."

"Grandfather says it isn't right for young people to oppose their parents and elders."

"That's just what I'd have expected Grandfather to say, and from now on I want you to bend your efforts toward forgetting every damn thing he ever told you."

Karel was silent for a while. "Mrs. Blumendahl, why is it wrong for a…for…" She swallowed and smiled miserably. "I guess I can't say it."

"That's because you're trying to doll it up. Say it like it is. You couldn't jar me if you concentrated on it."

She breathed deeply and made a fresh effort. "Grandfather knew that Jerry and I had…"

Fannie shrugged. "Oh, that! You want to know why it's wrong—if it is wrong?"

Karel moved uncomfortably. "It's supposed to be a sin, Grandfather says. Then he…"

"Sure he did, and as far as the act is concerned, he only acted like a man, but with *you* and the *way* he did it…" She made an angry noise in her throat. "Honey, do you believe in God?"

"I've always had to."

"I didn't ask what you had to do. Do you?"

Karel sighed, watching a squirrel that dashed across the road and scurried up a thick oak. "I don't know. I fought Grandfather's wishes—that is, deep down I did. Everything he told me I fought, and while fighting him, I did very little thinking of my own. So, I just don't know. Should I believe?"

"I'm not the one to tell you that," said Fannie crisply. "I, personally, do not believe that there is an old man with a beard who sits on high and frowns down on the very weaknesses he incorporated into humanity. I do not believe that one will go to hell for taking a drink or even for doing what you did with Jerry. The drink is harmless unless taken to excess, and the other is wrong only if *you* think it is. Even if you think so, you'd better examine your reasons carefully because no matter what you believe, your nature, your very human nature, is still there. It came along with you when you were born, but your beliefs are likely to be a hodge-podge of acquired impressions that *may* be good but are more likely all wet. Whatever good your grandfather taught you would be mighty suspect because of its source. Do you feel that what you and Jerry did was wrong?"

Karel did not immediately answer, seeming to be deep in thought.

"If you feel," said Fannie gently, "that I'll be sore at you if you say no to my question, then you can forget it. I won't."

"It isn't that," Karel pulled a leaf from an overhanging bough and crunched the stem in her strong white teeth. "I feel somehow—I don't know how or where I got the feeling—that if a man and a woman are in love, whatever way they choose to demonstrate that love is good."

"A very sound philosophy, my dear."

"And yet Jerry left me and never came back. He didn't love me and now I don't suppose I loved him because his leaving didn't make me sad for very long. Now it would seem that it was all wrong."

"No man, woman or child," said Fannie forcefully, "can see around the corner. One can only perform of and for the moment. If things show up in a different light the next day, who could have predicted it? Nothing is certain that depends on the future actions of people. Maybe in your philosophy you were wrong because of what subsequently happened, but since you couldn't possibly be expected to have known that, it would be the worst folly to become morbid and bang yourself about with censure."

Karel threw the leaf away, reached for another, missed and sat back with a smile. "Well, it is all I can do to keep from admitting that I liked it. I liked Jerry and what we did together, regardless of how I'm supposed to feel according to what other people think."

"Very well, admit it then. For God's sake, don't ever be false to yourself. You can't afford to be surgically honest with the public because of the heavy percentage of fools running loose in it, but you're a sunk schooner if you can't be honest with Karel."

Karel stretched her lovely legs straight in front of her and bore back against the seat. A smile of peace and relaxation touched her lips, not untinged with a certain sensuous satisfaction. "Okay, then I enjoyed it more than I ever did anything in my entire life."

"That's all right by me. I've been known to enjoy it a little myself." Fannie chuckled heavily, then sobered. "What would happen if I had a party and some good-looking skate pulled you off into the yard and tried to de-pants you?"

"I'd probably try to break his neck," said Karel firmly.

"Why?"

"Because—I know this might sound a little strange but— well, I couldn't fall in love that fast and unless I did, I'd certainly resent his putting his hands on me."

"Not even for a little mild necking?"

"Necking is fun, with kissing and things like that, but if it went any further, I'd resent it with some fast action. I think I know a little better what love is, now. Jerry was handsome, dashing—and unafraid of Grandfather. He attracted me because he was more of a grown man than the boys I've always known."

"Suppose you got pregnant?" asked Fannie with brutal bluntness. Karel slowly went pale.

"I suppose I never thought of that. I didn't think of much of anything at the time."

Fannie nodded vigorously. "Understandable, but still a risky thing. It could happen and I'm not telling you to scare you but to prepare you. Just remember to think of that in the future. I'm not going to tell you what you should or should not do either. You've had enough of that. I will tell you this though. Such things can be dangerous, as you must now appreciate, and once you're in the know, you have no one to blame but yourself if you get into trouble."

The girl shuddered. "I think you'll find that I'm not very smart...mother."

"No one is born smart...daughter." Fannie patted her leg affectionately. "We learn, usually, to whatever degree we are exposed to knowledge—and depending, of course, on our respective talents for learning."

"I failed at school," she murmured miserably.

"So did I. Three times. The crap they shove at you at school has been so miserably castrated and distilled that it's pretty poor pap at best. Somehow though, child, I'm sure you're going to be all right. If you had been one of those mealy mouthed "Look how nice I am" wenches who could shuck the pose come darkness like a hog shucks an ear of corn, then you'd have been on my list and I'd have bounced you off to boarding school if I couldn't have talked any sense into your head."

"Are you going to make me go to school?"

"I'm not going to make you do a blasted thing," stated Fannie flatly. "If you have any gumption, you'll get along without me barking at you all the time. If you haven't, all my shouting wouldn't do a cussed bit of good. If there's something you want to take up as a special course at some place where they go on the strength of intelligence and not diplomas, you can name your own poison. If you want to take a correspondence course in something, you can do it. If you want to stay with me and sit on your rump till some likable lad comes along and sucks you into marriage, then have at it."

"What have I done to deserve all this?" asked Karel with a touch of adolescent melodrama.

"Nothing, probably, and where did you read that phrase?"

The girl turned pink. "I sounded pretty bad, didn't I?"

"You sure did. We might ask what you had done to deserve the deal you got from your grandpop. Maybe this is just compensation for that. People rarely deserve what they get like you're getting this. It's what you do afterward that might tell the tale."

"But what can I do for you that would equal this?"

"*This*," said Fannie, "is a hell of a lot bigger to you than it is to me. I get a bang out of it, so if you are supporting any idea that I'm committing a sacrifice, forget it. I don't do things I don't want to do if I can possibly avoid it."

Something like a sighing sob welled from the girl's throat. "I'd still like to do something for you."

Fannie eleared her throat noisily. "Maybe someday you'll really love me. That would mean more to me than anything else."

"Oh, I do now! I do already." Karel flung her arms about the big woman and planted a soft, moist kiss on one plump cheek.

"Go on with you," bellowed Fannie, flustered badly. "Get your damn paws off me. I'll take your word for it." She fumbled for and found her cigarette holder and soon had a smoke going. "Don't pay any attention to me, sugar. I didn't mean to roar at you like that. You embarrassed me."

Karel let a tinkle of laughter escape from her lips. "Fannie, I think you're the hardest-acting, softest-hearted woman I ever saw, and I think I understand you perfectly."

Fannie grinned. "Then, dammit, don't go exposing me like that out of doors."

She pulled the horses to a plunging halt at the top of a hill. "There's your home, my dear, for as long as you want to stay."

Karel gasped, speechless before the wide panorama that was Fahenstock. The sun was setting in a sullen haze of vermillion dust, sending orange-red spears of light through the mighty trees that surrounded the majestic old house. The stained glass fanlight over the big front doors twinkled at them like a jewel. "Oh…" She put her hands to her face, her mouth open with amazed wonder. "I've heard of it. I've heard Grandfather speak of it as a den of iniquity but—"

"He would!"

"—but I never dreamed … and I'm going to *live* there?"

"That you are and now I'll bet you're starved. Mandy is having chicken pie tonight and until you've tasted Mandy's chicken pie, you ain't never et."

As Fannie Blumendahl had driven away with his granddaughter, the Reverend Rathborne had turned and slowly gone back into the empty, lifeless house, closing and bolting the door securely behind him. Wandering aimlessly from one dreary room to another, he had intoned commanding supplications to God, demanding justice and vengeance. Absently entering Karel's room, he had suddenly halted, stiffened and looked around him with something akin to fright.

"Karel?" he called tentatively. "Karel, they can't do this to me! God has spoken. What I did was good and right. It was right!" Frowning and standing still in the middle of the room, he seemed to be listening to unheard sounds. Then he let go an unearthly wail of anguish and began pacing the floor. "Karel!" he thundered. "Where are you, Karel? Come here. Come here at once. Disrobe! I will see for myself. Disrobe I say!" Breaking out in a clammy sweat, he fell face down on her bed, weeping wildly and crushing her pillow convulsively beneath his spasm-rocked, wretched body.

CHAPTER FIVE

ICK GAMBLE put his car up and walked along Main Street until he came to the Ford place. Business was shutting up for the day but Jeff Peters was at his desk, figuring laboriously with a pencil, the point of which was in his mouth more than it was on the paper. He looked up.

"Come in, son. Find a place to stay and get all bedded down?"

Dick walked over to the desk. "Maybe I bedded down too soon."

"How come?"

Dick related the events of the afternoon without skimping any of the details. Jeff Peters put his pencil down. "I got a daughter that I think a lot of. She's a good gal but headstrong, and the way she and Janey Hardwicke hates each other is almost always funny to everybody. Sometimes it gets past bein' funny, such as like now. See here, I gave you a job. Long as you satisfy me, you got a job, Annette or no Annette. You'll get raises as fast as time and talent'll get 'em for you. That satisfactory?"

Dick felt a warm rush of affection for the old man. He appeared to be so fat and helpless, and he was probably badgered unmercifully by his daughter. There was, however, steel when steel was needed. Dick was not a man to display his feelings though, and he nodded carelessly.

"That's good enough for me. I'll do any man's work for him but I'll be damned if I'll bend a knee to his folks."

He left and walked down into the main block of town where he entered a barroom and ordered a beer. It was cold and its tang felt good. Just as he began to relax, shrill female voices from outside drew his attention to the window. With an exclamation of disbelief, he put down his beer mug and ran to the wide door. There on the sidewalk, ringed by a group of amused spectators, Annette Peters and Janey Hardwicke were violently engaged in a hair-pulling contest. They were screaming and kicking viciously at each other, lurching back and forth across the pavement, their faces red and twisted with anger and pain.

"Third time this month," said Abe Mullins, wiping his hands on his apron as he came to watch over Dick's shoulder.

Dick grinned. "Two to one on Annette."

"I'll take you. How much?"

"A fiver."

"Okay. It's a deal."

At that point Janey threw a sudden haymaker that struck Annette beneath the ear and deposited her in a skidding sprawl against the Post Office building. Several onlookers took advantage of the lull to place the girls forcibly—kicking, squealing and flailing—in their respective cars. Dick turned back to his beer, depositing a ten-dollar bill on the counter for Abe.

"Well, I'll be," he said. "I've seen less and paid more."

Abe snorted. "That weren't nothin'. I seen 'em do a better job of it once. Janey got knocked down first and pulled Annette with her. You never seen the like of legs and drawers in your born days. Both of 'em got the best-lookin' meat in town."

"You're probably right," replied Dick with a chuckle. "The winner I've seen before—and I know she's a knockout."

A man whom Dick had not noticed walked up and tapped him forcefully on the shoulder. Dick faced about, his jaw muscles tightening with irritation.

"What was that you said, neighbor?" demanded the stranger.

Before Dick could answer, Abe whacked the bar resoundingly with a bungstarter. "If you got trouble on your mind, Jack, take it sommers else."

"Just stay on your side of the bar, fat man, and you won't have any trouble. I asked you what it was you said." He turned again to Dick, prodding him hard in the solar plexus. Dick, whose temper was always of notable brevity, suddenly went into action with such explosive violence that the man and two chairs struck the floor simultaneously. The fallen gladiator lay still.

"How many times didja hit 'im?"

"Twice."

"Coulda swore it but I didn't see neither one of 'em. Guess Mr. Jack is a mite surprised. A bully sort of and a queer Joe if I ever seen one."

"He must be an idiot. What the hell's the matter with him?"

"I think he is hopeful in terms of Janey. A far piece behind the pack and not too pleased about it. I plumb fergot he was in here. Guess we stepped on him where his toes hurt."

"Who is he?"

"Jack McGrew. Old family, lazy, not much money, lotsa background that he can't spend."

"That's enough out of you, Abe," said Jack, coming off the floor. "As for you, Mister, I'm going to tell you what's the matter with me. Then I'm going to damn well kill you."

"How?" asked Dick with deliberate insolence. "Bushwhack me, shoot me, or carve me up with a knife?"

McGrew opened his huge hands and spread them wide. "With these, neighbor."

Abe opened his mouth to protest, then saw the smooth-muscled coordination with which Dick swung clear of the bar and grinned, settling himself back against the counter with folded arms. Jack moved in with slow deliberation, suddenly swinging a terrific right that Dick ducked neatly. So powerful was the force of the blow that Jack was pulled off balance and fell to the floor with a crash that made bottles and glasses dance.

Abe leaned chummily over the bar. "Another'n like that, Mr. Jack, and you will win your own fight fer ... fer ... er ... what's your name, pardner?"

"Dick Gamble. Say, is this bird all right in the head?"

"Some says he is and others says he ain't. Right now I agrees with them that says he ain't, cause he's comin' off that floor in a second askin' fer more."

Where the man got the beer bottle and where he hid it until he threw it is still an unsolved mystery. Dick's reactions were not quite quick enough and it caught him flush on a cheek bone, exploding and shattering into a thousand pieces. Abe sucked in his cheeks and grasped his bungstarter. With a leap that belied his weight, he cleared the bar just as Jack, with an animal-like sound, aimed a kick at the head of the unconscious Dick. The hardwood mallet cracked dully and Jack slid to the floor, his hands clenching and unclenching spasmodically. Abe snorted noisily and waddled to the back of the bar where he picked up the telephone. "Gimme the Clinic."

Three minutes later a long white ambulance skidded to a stop before the saloon, the siren grinding out a dying, throaty moan.

"I ain't taking care of no more of your drunks—Jesus, what happened?" Happy Olsen scratched his head.

"Mr. Jack there got tapped on the conk. This gent here—Dick Gambler or something like that, I think he said—got hit in the face with a beer bottle. Better take 'im in."

Happy knelt and examined the patients briefly. "Nasty gash this young feller's got here in the face. Mr. Jack is all right. I never seen your bungstarter cause a fracture yet—less you're slippin'."

"I give him my five minute dose. He'll come to d'reckly. I called about this young feller. He got a nasty lick."

"Guess I'll take him around to Dr. Franchette. Dr. Jenkins is got the evenin' off and Dr. Albert is tied up with a woman what's ten days over her time. He's busy."

"Take him sommers. He's amessin' up my floor."

Dr. Franchette held his gloved hands out to Maude, who stripped them expertly from his thin, sensitive fingers. "You may sit up, young man—that is, if you feel up to it. You might be a little woozy yet."

Dick sat, and in another five minutes, with two ounces of Bradsher's Special Age tingling in his stomach, he felt almost equal to taking on more belligerence. Dr. Franchette, cuddling a highball of fearful proportions, sat opposite him and watched the blood come back to his face.

"You had a nasty cut," he said gently. "Took eleven stitches and fished out a couple of bullets of brown glass. You have an orange-slice fracture of the cheek bone, but since there was no displacement, it'll be all right."

"Orange slice..." His tongue felt thick and his face seemed ballooned out of shape.

"That's right. It's a sort of break where the separations converge to an axis—cheek bone. Nothing to worry about."

"What about that Jack somebody-or-other?"

"Oh, Happy said Abe chilled him with a mallet. I'm going to have to look him up one of these days."

"I should think so," said Dick. "The man is nuts."

"He's getting to be dangerous."

"What's the matter with him? I mean, is he really insane?"

"Hard to define, son. He's young, spoiled, dipsomaniac mother-hovered, introverted and a coward at heart, although I dislike the term. He tries to cover it up by attacking smaller men. He has a formidable array of victories."

"They must all be blind and deaf. He couldn't hit the ground with his hat."

"He seemed to have had perfect aim with a bottle."

"Didn't expect it. He said he was going to kill me with his bare hands. I take a lot of killing." A look of granite stubbornness came to his face and the Doctor squinted at him.

"You know, your face has an awfully familiar cast. What did you say your name was?"

"Gamble, Sir. Phillip Richard Gamble—Junior."

Franchette burst into a staccato chuckle that made his spade beard dance. "Did your father ever mention Theodore Franchette to you?"

The boy's head went up. "Theodore Franchette—you mean the one who helped him stuff that cannon on the campus full of black powder and paper, set it off and break all the windows in the zoology lab?"

Dr. Franchette's white teeth gleamed in a grin of satanic reminiscence. "The same. A good fellow, Dick Gamble, when he finally got sense enough to let me make the plans. That cannon deal didn't come out in all the details for twenty years. By that time, nothing could be done about it."

Dick felt gingerly of his face. "Dad died a few years back, Doctor—ten, to be exact. I suppose you knew?"

Franchette nodded soberly. "I knew, but too late to do anything but write your poor mother a letter of sympathy. And of course, before she got it, she was in her grave also." They sat in silence for a moment. "And now," said the Doctor briskly, "what are you doing here?"

"I'm going to work tomorrow at the Ford place."

Franchette nodded without enthusiasm. "Peters is rough but a good man. He won't ride you."

"You don't seem to be enthusiastic."

"I'm not. Why aren't you a doctor like your father?"

The boy's face hardened. "Because Dad tried to make me into one."

The other nodded. "I know—his father tried to make a forester out of him, so he studied medicine. Where does this streak of perverseness come into your family?"

"What does it matter? Do you consider a parent's wish a good enough reason for taking up medicine—or anything else, for that matter?"

"No, not necessarily. By the way, what sort of degree did you take at the University?"

"Er …" Dick looked out of the window. "Forestry."

"Remarkable," murmured the Doctor. "A pattern seems to have formed. Do you like medicine?"

"Very much, sir … that is, no. No, I don't like it at all." Dick's face reddened.

"Ummm, I see. Well, any time you feel like talking and have a load of some opaque material in your craw, come to see me again."

"Opaque?"

"Certainly. Right at this moment you are as transparent as Chicago coffee."

Dick couldn't meet the bright, button-like eyes and, standing, he pulled out a billfold. "How much do I owe you?"

"Not a penny. I'm half retired anyway. My son, Albert, was busy or they'd have taken you to the Clinic."

"I'd much prefer to pay my own way." Dick's voice was hostile and stiff.

"What the hell do I care what you prefer?" exploded the fiery little Doctor. "Go on about your business, and if you feel that you must give your money away, find some cute wench and give it to her. Maybe she'll give you something in return."

Dick left the house in embarrassed confusion, his ears burning and his palms wet. In the years since the war he had been able to awe people with his attitude of uncompromising inflexibility. The Doctor had turned on him like a fighting cock, leaving him floundering and feeling ridiculous. Franchette's sudden questions had surprised things from him that he did not want to reveal. He clenched his hands against the prod of his bruised vanity, and feeling a little weak and headachy, he headed back toward the boarding house.

News travels fast in a small community, and he found Mrs. Pinkney waiting with advice, assorted chatter and an ice bag. He took the ice bag and politely but firmly shut the door on the others. After an hour his cheek felt almost normal, and when he heard the scratching on his window, he was alert and awake. Remembering the savage, unbridled fury in the eyes of the man he had encountered earlier in the afternoon, he did not go to the window but opened a pair of French doors that looked out on a terrace, stepped through them and peered around the corner of the house. In the brilliant moonlight he could see the slim figure of Janey Hardwicke standing on tiptoes to scratch on his window with a branch.

"Looking for someone?"

With a startled gasp she whirled about and, coming toward him, her smooth hips rose and fell with exaggerated cat-like grace beneath a soft white dress that clung like wet silk to every inch it covered.

"You scared me," she said with a throaty little laugh, coming on until she stood close to him. He was clad in thin pajama shorts and nothing else, but if he was self-conscious, he did not show it. Taking one final step toward him, she inched her body so close to his that involuntarily he opened his arms and took her into an embrace.

She avoided his lips with another low laugh and slipped out of his arms to sit on the stone steps of the terrace. "You scared me," she said again.

"Twice in one day?"

"That isn't fair, Dick, and look at what you made me do."

"I'll admit that I didn't know I was going to scare you that badly. But that's the way it goes—country girls with pseudo-sophisticated ideas cave in and shove when the chips are down, even forgetting their clothes. Nice haymaker you swung this afternoon."

Her jaw tightened. "That little bitch! Telling all those people that she saw me running with no clothes on from a man."

"Well, the 'no clothes' was a slight exaggeration, but the rest was rather painfully true, wasn't it?"

She shrugged. "Why can't we forget it and go on from here? I've squelched that little rumor once and for all."

"So now it's a rumor?" He chuckled.

"What are you doing tonight?"

"Right now I'm thinking of going to bed. Your champion, Jack something-or-other, tried to do me in."

She sneered. "That imbecile. I heard you laid him flat and it serves him right. I'm sorry about your wound. I can scarcely see it in this light." She laid cool fingers on his face in a caress that made his spine tingle.

"Tell me," he asked seriously, "do all Kenton girls take after a new man as hard as you and Annette do?"

Her smile was distant and knowing. "Maybe we think of it as a game. Our apparent speed is a means of beating the other to the goal line."

"Fascinating. The men must love it except when they're getting the run-around." She was silent and he continued. "What did you have in mind for tonight—a cross buck mouse trap where the opposing tackle is sucked through an empty hole and blocked while the play switches and goes over his vacant position?"

She made a little face at him and chuckled. "Something like that, possibly."

"Well, I'd better warn you. I used to be a sucker for that play until I caught on, and now I can spot one a mile off."

"You play too seriously, Dick," she said with a slight frown.

"You don't really mean that. What you mean is that I don't fall into the trap with calf eyes all agoo with lahve and give away all the details of my clumsy strategy. Nope, I think I'll try Annette's brand of play. She interests me."

A spasm flashed across Janey's face but was controlled instantly. "Do you have a date?"

"No."

"Then why worry about her? I'm right next door, I have an excellent cellar and my folks are away for two weeks." Her eyes beckoned to him hotly.

He stood up. "My face feels so good now that I think a few drinks might make it feel normal. Wait for me. I'll be only a few seconds." Returning, dressed in soft flannels and a white sport shirt, he said, "Lead me to the cellar. I crave flagons of Bacardi with a small Coke chaser on the side and a touch of lime to liven it."

"It shall be just as you desire," she said, sweeping him a low bow that revealed the satiny skin and smoothly flowing muscles of her back where the dress was cut away.

The Hardwicke living room was of a rococo vintage but the chairs and couches were comfortable and deep. Janey put a coffee table before the couch and placed a loaded tray upon it. She had provided Bacardi, Coke, limes, ice, a bottle of Teachers' for herself and a siphon of soda. She poured a drink for him that had 'mickey' tagged all over it. Her own drink was a modest tablespoonful with ice and a dash of soda.

He had to have a knife with which to cut the lime and while she was gone, he added a stiff jolt of Scotch to her drink and was gratified to see, when she tasted it, that she didn't seem to notice. His own drink he sipped slowly, making it last a long time.

"Drink up," she said gaily. "I've had two."

"With a tablespoonful each time. You pour out half a glass of this cane juice for me and call it even." He gazed at the liquor left in his glass. "Tell you what. You pour out just half that amount of Scotch and I'll bottoms-up with you."

"Okay, Simon Legree. You never let a girl get ahead of you."

"That's my motto. Cheerio."

"Prosit."

She grimaced and chased the stiff drink with a sip of Coke. "I don't like to drink like that."

"Don't do it then. At the same time, you might let me take my time. After all, I have a job to go to in the morning."

Janey fixed fresh drinks and they danced for a while. Later he again spiked her drink heavily when she left the room for a moment and again she didn't notice it. And while she fiddled with the radio, he pretended to read the label on the bottle and, for the third time, he let another extra charge slide into her drink. Janey's eyes began to shine brightly and her laugh took on a new lilt—strident and raucous, not the controlled coo that she had been careful to modulate. She flopped on the couch, her skirt flying up, giving him a glance of smooth, elegantly tanned thighs. Feeling that she was sufficiently tight, he gradually closed the distance between them.

"Dick, don't look at me like that." She moistened her lips with her tongue until they shone wetly.

"What do you mean?"

"Like that, like you're doing now."

"Why not?"

"Because ... because you're frightening me again."

She sought to avoid his lips but he was too quick for her. For a long moment she resisted him stiffly, her hands trying to push him away, her head twisting this way and that in her effort to escape his mouth. He did not relent but rather held her closer until, exhausted, she gradually subsided. Rubbing her back in smooth circles of rhythm, he pressed her against him until her pointed breasts were firm against his chest. His persistent mouth parted her lips and his tongue hotly caressed their inner wet slickness. Releasing her slightly, he buried his face in her neck and one hand cupped and lifted a ripe, throbbing breast.

"No, Dick ... Oh, Dick, I can't stand it! Please!" Again his lips stopped her and the hot stab of her tongue told a story of its own. He slipped the scanty dress off her shoulders and, lifting her slightly, he pulled it down her body in one swift motion.

"Dick..." It was a mumble that her own lips drowned in their efforts to fuse with his again. Pulling him with her, she fell back against the couch, her eyes closed tight, her breath heaving wildly. "Oh, Dick, we can't," she said, at the same time straining toward him. "Please stop us...I've never...really, I haven't...don't let it happen."

"This time you can't run," he said fiercely.

Her breath cut off suddenly and for a moment there was not a sound in the room. Gradually, gradually he had his way until suddenly a sharp cry of shock rent the air—that breathless, exultant gasp of the female, rich music to the ear of every conquering male through the ages. It was the cue before full orchestration and then the sounds of Nature herself swelled the air— the whacking sounds of hungry flesh meeting flesh, the strains of strutted tendon, the sleek rub of muscle pulling together, the smacking sounds of wetness, tender sounds, rough sounds...so unds...sounds...sounds.

Later she covered his lips with her hot, damp mouth, serpent like, enticing and devouring him like a starving woman. "Oh, Dick..." She strained him to her in a sudden excess of tender passion. "Oh, Dick, I love you so."

"Don't forget the game, my dear," he said coolly as he stroked the tender skin of her flank.

"Oh, how can you bring that up now?" She found his mouth and buried her own. "Dick?"

"Yes."

"Do you love me?"

"No man can enjoy what I just had and not love the woman. It's mathematical."

"But some don't."

"Some can't ever reach the heights. They just stumble along and never know what a crescendo is."

"But we know, don't we?" she whispered, taking him in an embrace that made him sit up.

"There must be a better place in this house."

She got up slowly, reluctant to lose contact with him for even a moment. "Will you carry me?"

He grinned. "Men always do in books, so why not now?"

Some time later he left her sleeping wth a laxity that can stem from but a single cause, pulled the door shut behind him and sought his own bed.

CHAPTER SIX

JUST HOW many yards of chiffon went into one of Fannie Blumendahl's party dresses was never known to any degree of exactitude. One man had been heard to whisper that he had seen a 75mm pack howitzer dropped from a plane during the war and the 'chute would, he guessed, approximate the yardage of one of Fannie's dresses. Tonight, as she prepared to dress, she was happier than usual because this party was rather special. It was summer, which always meant an influx of visiting firemen, and she hoped one at least might prove to be a man whose mettle would entitle him to call on Karel.

The dress in question lay draped voluminously over a chair while Lula and Bessie, her two maids, sweated and tugged vigorously at various straps and laces by which they strove to compress Fannie's two-hundred-plus poundage into a more dressable size.

"Hooly! Dammit, Lula, you caught a piece of meat that time as big as a sirloin ... let off, Bessie, or you'll bust the thing. Then I'll be in a hell of a fix. Now wait ... wait. Let's have some team-work in this thing. I'm going to hold my breath like this ... see? Then, when I wave my hand, you both pull to beat hell—get it?" Bessie and Lula giggled and nodded their heads. "All right now, here we go." Fannie held her breath and the two maids pulled with all their might, making the laces and straps fast and step-ping out of range as though afraid of an explosion. For a moment there was no sound but Fannie's face gradually grew purple and a strangling bleat came from between her lips. She motioned to them frantically but before they could come to her aid, an entire side of the corset gave way, ripping out eyelets and exploding rivets like the plates of a rammed ship.

"Whoooie! Holy balls of catfish! What I don't go through with to look pretty for those jerks who come to my parties. Bessie, dig into that closet and see if there isn't another corset in there. My old one should be there. I told that fool of a clerk this damn thing would bust out at the seams like a wet sack. Lula, what the hell are you laughing at? By God, I'll scalp you. Go tell Miss Karel to come here."

When the girl arrived, Fannie had at last been crammed into restraint that showed fairly good signs of holding. She wiped the sweat from her brow and sat down at the dressing table.

"Come in, sugar, I..." As she spoke, she turned around and the girl entered, dressed in pale green taffeta faille. The dress was simple and cut low to the point of severity. Her creamy shoulders were richly luminous in the soft light and her hair foamed over her ears to tumble in orderly profusion at the base of her neck. Her sea-green eyes sparkled and green crystal pendants danced from her ears as she walked.

"Why in the name of Beelzebub do I bother to dress when I have you around?" demanded Fannie. "No matter what I do, you make me look worse than Lula after a jag on a muddy night." Bessie and Lula smothered their mirth and averted their faces.

Karel, her face alight with joy, spun around so rapidly that the full skirt flared and unveiled her long bare legs. "You like it?" She was breathlessly expectant.

"Sugar, you're a dream. You ain't so. I don't believe it."

The girl suddenly stopped her posturing and slid to her knees and, seizing one of Fannie's hands, kissed it fervently. "Oh, Fannie, I've never been so happy in all my life—in all my life."

Fannie cleared her throat loudly. "Look here, now. None of this blubbering. You'll ruin your make-up."

Karel looked up, her breasts heaving, her eyes a-swim with tears, but her smile was wide, if somewhat tremulous. "But I don't have any on—just lipstick."

"Well…Here, let me see. Dog my cats, you sure don't," Fannie sighed. "There was a day when I didn't use makeup either but that's long gone. Hey! Lula, what're you trying to do—scalp me?"

On this particular night Fannie had gone over her lists with great care and the crowd was hand-picked. The McAlisters were there and so were the Peters, the Melvins, the Ackers, the McGrews, the Ponsenbys, as well as a sprinkling of the cream of St. Louis Parish society over on the river—the Saltons, the Pickwicks, the Strudwicks and the Williamsons.

"I don't care what anyone says," averred Mrs. Melvin to Mrs. Acker and Mrs. McGrew. "If Fannie took her in, she's all right. I don't know how she managed to get her out of the clutches of that old—"

Mrs. McGrew drew herself up haughtily. "Have a care, Jessica. The Reverend Rathborne is the very soul of nobility, the breath of upright Christianity."

"Oh, come," countered Edna Acker. "The man is a tyrant and a fool. Why do you feel called upon to defend him?"

"Because I will not stand idly by and see a man of God maligned and not raise a hand. I have heard it whispered that there was some collusion between old Dr. Franchette and Fannie. As for that old rake of a Doctor, why do you know, he actually *leered* at me not a week ago?"

"I understand—though it's probably not true, of course" said Edna, her lips stiff with resentment, "that he saved your Jack's leg when it was nearly cut off in that car wreck and that he didn't charge you a penny. You know how lies like that get started."

Mrs. McGrew's not unattractive face went so dark with embarrassed blood that her make-up seemed as white as flour. She made a muttered excuse and moved away, looking with spurious intensity for someone with whom she affected to have pressing business.

"Well, Edna," chortled Mrs. Melvin, "you certainly put a screw in *her* clock. She'll hate you, my dear."

"Who cares? I'll put a screw in anyone else's clock who talks about Dr. Franchette. He's one of the very few men in the parish who are worth their salt. I wish he'd leer at *me*."

Fannie, while all this friendly repartee was going on, was in her little study immediately off the ballroom talking animatedly over the telephone. She never excused herself when she left her assembly—she merely walked away and people chuckled and said how just like Fannie it was.

"But look, you broken-down old scavenger, you know very damned well I don't give a hoot in hell if you come to a party of mine—but I want to know why you want to come. Usually wild horses couldn't drag you."

"If," countered Dr. Franchette acidly, "a man of my age and stature wants to attend a party, why shouldn't he be allowed to do so without all this third degree?"

"Oh, very well, come ahead and bring all your blasted mystery with you... Oh!" Fannie stopped with tooth-aching suddenness. Her voice slipped so far down in volume when she spoke again that Franchette could hardly hear her. "I'm so sorry, Theodore. Oh, my God, how could I be so thick? Of course, you wanted to see her her first night out." She sniffed audibly. "Come on out and please try to forgive me. I guess I'm just an old fool. It never entered my mind."

"You have been an old fool for more years than I'm cruel enough to mention," he snapped. "I'll be there in half an hour."

"I'll be looking for you," she said with such meekness that she barked like a seal as soon as she had cradled the receiver, angry at the unaccustomed and embarrassing predicament in which she had put herself.

Lula put her head in the door. "Did you call me, Miss Fannie?"

"No, I didn't call you, and get the hell out of my sight before I throw a vase at you." Lula giggled and withdrew but fragments of Fannie's trumpeting voice had filtered out into the assembly.

"I wonder who that is," lisped Miss Martha Strudwick, an elderly spinster whose activities consisted principally of the destruction of good bourbon whiskey and the propagation of Siamese cats.

"Some drunken servant, no doubt," offered Mrs. Alyce Williamson, a divorcée whose days of gaiety, had there ever been any, were on the wane. "I'm surprised that Fannie would have her about."

Jefferson Salton, who knew Fannie well, hid his face in his drink and made a bubbling sound, drawing attention to the fact that he was red with suppressed mirth. He turned around and moved away to safer quarters, his broad shoulders shaking.

Fannie entered the magnificently decorated ballroom where her guests either chattered in cliquish knots, drank from the endless store of whiskey or ate from the groaning tables. With regal splendor and dulcet tones, she dispensed favors, dropping a quick phrase here, a sweet smile or a roguish wink, waving her chiffon scarf gracefully, daring not to breathe too deeply or make a sudden, quick gesture. Fannie had never burst a gusset in public, but she lived in constant fear of it.

Karel, who had been cornered by every unattached male in the place, either singly or en masse, had disappeared for a breath of air and, sneaking back into the big room, she strove to avoid their searching eyes. None of them had attracted her and she found their attentions uniformly irritating and their wolfish smirks revolting. Suddenly she came face to face with Fannie, who was talking to old Mrs. Pickwick.

"My dear," cooed Fannie, "you look simply adorable in that black sheer. I can always depend on you to exhibit the most beautiful taste. If I were as trim as you, I'd wear nothing but black sheer." Mrs. Pickwick, who could match Fannie pound for pound and still come out ahead, fairly wriggled with pleasure. "Oh, thank you, Mrs. Blumendahl. I always love your parties. I've always told my husband that of all the hostesses we know, you are by far the best, haven't I, 'Lonzo, dear?"

Alonzo Pickwick, who was searching in the depths of his glass for a cherry which he was mortally certain still reposed there, nodded absently. "Why, of course, my sugarplum."

Fannie then saw Karel staring at her through large, shocked and unbelieving eyes.

"Have fun, you lovely people," cooed Fannie and, grasping Karel by the arm, she hustled her into the study.

"Dammit, honey, why were you staring at me like that? Didn't you know I was two people—maybe even three or four? I'm one to you and to my friends. To those frantic cattle out there, I'm quite another." Karel appeared about to burst from mirth, making Fannie squirm uncomfortably. "What the hell's so damned funny?"

Karel whipped a green scarf languidly over her wrist. "Oh, deah Fannie…how I just lahve your pahties."

Fannie turned pink but laughed. "Don't worry, honey. I know how silly it sounds and I get as big a kick out of it as you do. That's why I give these damn shindigs. You know now so don't be gawking at me and exposing me before all those people—I got a reputation to uphold."

Dr. Franchette arrived on schedule and was ushered through private channels to the study. Fannie and Karel entered a few minutes later, causing the Doctor to bounce to his feet and stare at the girl in wonder. "*Magnifique!*" he breathed ecstatically. "My dear, you are lovely. You make me regret my years."

"For a man of your years," put in Fannie, "that should be a full-time job."

Karel battled the lump in her throat for a moment and then ran to him, putting her cheek against his weathered jowl.

"I wish there was some way I could thank you both. I can't, so you'll just have to do with all my love. I told Fannie that she had that for as long as I live. That goes for you, too."

"Pooh," said Fannie carelessly. "More melodrama."

"Well, child, I'll live to regret saying this, but you couldn't have picked a finer mother for yourself—not if you hunted the world over."

Fannie's eyes began to blur and she cleared her throat loudly, fumbling in a desk drawer for a bottle which she produced, flourished and put on a small table. "First thing we know, we'll all be sobbing on each other's chest. Let's inject some humor and festivity." She put the bottle away, shaking her head. "Nope, I'll call Lula to bring up some bubble water." She did and they toasted each other with fine old champagne.

Dr. Franchette put down his glass and turned to Karel. "There's a man I want you to meet."

She raised her dark brows. "I thought I'd met everyone here."

"This one just arrived. I saw him come in when I did, but he didn't see me. He's the son of an old classmate of mine. If you don't like him, just smile, bow and let it go at that. You two stay here and I'll fetch him if I don't get tangled in that web of fluttering women out there."

"They'll let you go as soon as they see what they've caught," jibed Fannie raucously.

Dick Gamble found himself at Fannie's party through a set of circumstances with which he had had little to do. A dead battery in his car gave him a perfect alibi when Annette coyly suggested that he take her to Fannie Blumendahl's party. He produced his alibi with such casual assurance that Jeff Peters, mistaking his tone for one of depression, instantly offered him the pick of the used-car lot for the night. Dick accepted Jeff's offer for two reasons—he intended to make the drive back home with Annette a profitable one, and he did not want to offend Jeff, who was generous and openhearted, genuinely desiring to do him a favor.

The party, with it's heterogeneous collection of dowagers, misty-faced adolescents, wolves and crochety husbands, bored him to insensibility. As a result, he was such poor company that Annette, in a fit of pique, left him to his own devices and flounced away in search of game. He found a secluded corner occupied by a deep, inviting chair, and after fortifying himself with a long drink, he sat down to watch and wish that he was at home in bed.

It was there that Dr. Franchette found him. "Ah, there, Richard. Am I intruding?"

"No indeed, Doctor. I'm glad to see you. I've been so bored I could scream. What's so great about these parties?"

"That fact that Fannie Blumendahl gives them."

Dick made a gesture of distaste. "I dislike social empresses."

"You won't dislike her. She's not the usual kind of a social empress at all. In fact, she admits that she gives her parties so people will come and perform for her. She enjoys it hugely."

"That sounds better. I've been watching and, taken from that angle, they do perform amusingly. I saw a man pinch a woman on the behind a while ago and she giggled and squeezed his hand. I'm mortally certain she was not his wife."

"And I am, too," agreed the Doctor. "To what purpose would a man pinch his wife's fanny?"

Dick laughed and lit a cigarette. "Wife or not, there was certainly a lot of it to pinch."

"What have you seen tonight that would interest you?" asked the Doctor, tasting a drink he had picked up on the way.

"Nothing," said Dick shortly, "except, of course, what I brought with me. She should be better after we leave."

Franchette frowned and Dick noticed it. "Do I shock you?"

"Oh, no." He put the glass down. "I'm shock-proof, son. I was just wondering what your attitude was toward women, generally."

"Love 'em," said Dick airily. "Love all of 'em. The more cooperative they are, the more I love 'em."

"You never met one whom you did not see in terms of ... er ... this cooperation?"

"Oh, sure—before I had any better sense." His tone was bitter. "I put her on a pedestal, I worshipped her. I would have rubbed my forehead on her feet except that I was afraid I'd soil them."

"Extremes," murmured the Doctor, lighting a cheroot.

"What?"

"Extremes. You leap from one extremity to the other. Haven't you ever heard of a middle road?"

"Sure. Lots of times. I never found it, though."

"It's time you did. You're not a callow, beardless youth any more, Richard."

"Are you telling me that my reactions are those of a youth?"

"Precisely, except that few youths go even as far as you have. You're being transparent again. Some girl treads on your toes and, whammo, you want to get back at her by roughing up practically every woman you see whom you consider worthy of your mettle. Scarcely the reaction of a mature, integrated man."

Dick slumped back in the chair and hid his face behind his highball. Franchette had begun a train of thought when they first met, a train that kept getting more uncomfortable the further it was traveled. This last remark of his was hardly an improvement.

"Nevertheless," said the Doctor, puffing rapidly, "there is a girl here I'd like for you to meet—just as a favor to me. You will not be obligated to cultivate her."

Dick put his glass down, feeling a curious resentment of which he was more than half ashamed. "Nothing to lose there, I suppose. Lead on and I shall follow with every evidence of no anticipation."

"Anticipation is ever greater than realization," quoth the little man, and they crossed the room that hummed with noisy chatter and brittle laughter as alcohol began to make its headway. Dr. Franchette opened the door to the study and ushered Dick in.

"Miss Snowden, may I present Mr. Richard Gamble?"

Karel murmured acknowledgement and Dick bowed and said, "How do you do?" He shook hands with Fannie and marveled at the grip of her hand. They talked desultorily for a while before Dick, feeling uncomfortable, made his apologies and withdrew to the anonymous protection of the ballroom.

"I'd hardly call him a bargain," grumbled Fannie. "Nice enough looking, holds himself well, but—"

"He's unhappy," said Karel with quiet conviction.

Franchette shot her a keen glance. "How do you know that?"

She shrugged. "I probably couldn't tell you. Maybe it was his absent-minded...I mean his mechanical way of...I really couldn't say. He looked at me and never saw me. He was being polite but he was bored before he ever came in here. Fannie, I'm tired. May I go to bed?"

"Certainly, dear. Go ahead. I'll make apologies for you."

Dr. Franchette sipped his drink with fastidious relish and pulled at his beard. "The child has instinct, whatever that is."

"Amen...what is it?"

"I don't know, but I do know she took a two-second look at Dick Gamble and plugged him right smack in the proper hole."

Dick succeeded in enticing Annette away from the party, and after enduring a slightly alcoholic tirade dealing intimately with his shortcomings as an escort, his resemblance to a flat tire and his utter lack of taste in having anything at all to do with Janey Hardwicke, he stopped trying to reason with her and drove along in complete silence, letting her blow without any comeback. After a time she grew tired of it, as he had known she would, and cuddled up close to him.

"I'm sorry I was mean," she said after her cuddling drew no response from him. Dick said nothing but stared stonily ahead of him.

"I said I was sorry."

"I heard you."

"But you don't believe me."

"It makes no difference one way or the other."

She brooded over this for a minute. "Why are you so cold and distant?"

"Because if I was hot and near at hand, it'd be hotter than you could stand and you'd run screaming to papa."

"How do you know I would?"

"Janie did."

"I'm certainly not Janey. Dick, you talk about things so flatly and don't let a girl ... I mean ..."

"You mean that I'm straightforward and don't let a girl hide behind anything. Why should she?"

"Well, girls have pride, you know."

Dick gave a single bark of derisive laughter and swung the car off the road onto a narrow, unused trail.

"Where are you going?"

"I don't know. I'm just headed some place since you've decided to be decent company."

He was traveling at a crawl as the trail wound deviously through the deep woods and finally he stopped the car in the center of a little clearing where a late moon cast pale light over a thick carpet of short grass.

Annette, acting as she had acted with men before, put her arms behind her and stretched, her legs straight in front of her, stomach drawn in and breasts surging against their restraint.

A charge of salty saliva flooded his mouth, making him swallow quickly.

"I can't see why all this rivalry between you and Janey. You could beat her any way in the book."

Annette smiled smugly. "You think so?"

"I'm certain of it."

"Why do you fool with her then?"

He lifted a careless shoulder. "I had to know. I never go by surface manifestations only."

"That's all you have to go by with me."

"That's what you think."

"I don't get it."

"You will soon." He grabbed her roughly and drew her across his lap, cradling her head in his left arm. Then he slowly bent forward and kissed her. She lay lax for a moment before, with a gasp, adding her own activities to the game, the zeal of which made Dick take startled notice. This, he told himself, should provide amusement—probably more than had Janey, although of the latter he had no complaint. Annette drew away from him as though in fear, but when he did not press his advantage, she rearranged her hair, smiled and glanced at him. "Now who's a sissy?"

"You. You were just before hollering for papa."

With a quick sinuous flip, she flung herself across him and encircled his neck with her arms, her dress climbing unnoticed or ignored, making available to Dick a moon-washed leg that set his pulses to hammering. He smiled inwardly and kissed her again, surpassing his first effort by minutes and finesse. When he released her, she was gasping, her eyes wide with a depth that seemed to rob them of expression. Her breath fluttered uncertainly and she sat up, drawing away from him, shaking her head hard.

"Sissy." He dropped the one word with contempt.

"No." A hard rigor possessed her. "No...I don't think..." She gripped her face with her hands for a moment and so did not see his advance that crushed her into an embrace before she had a chance to resist. A zipper grated in the still air. Her muscles bunched hard in resistance that did not include motion, a resistance of will but no offense. His hands roved expertly to her back, made short work of the catch of her brassiere, and a gasping cry struggled from her throat as his hands cupped her. The shot-hard tip of her breast was like a charged wire to the tip of his tongue, while her efforts to aid him made a delightfully fragrant mask for his face, fitting with firm, smothering, warm, trembling flesh, throbbing with the hammer-like blows of her heart. His hands roved over her body, pitching her into fever-ish excitement, a-quiver from the delicacy of his caress and the flood of upsurging passion it released. He felt her sharp teeth on his neck and shoulder, heard her hot breath whimpering pleas, incoherent endearments.

She did not protest the loss of her dress nor that of her more intimate garments but she insisted that he face the world in a like state and that she be allowed to perform the operation.

Suddenly Dick pushed her away and got out of the car, lean-ing against the cold, hard surface of a fender. Annette collapsed sobbing on the seat. "Don't go…Dick…come back…come back!"

He said nothing, looking out through the dark woods, seemingly calm to her because she could not see him properly, but seething like a cauldron, deliberately forcing himself to punish her—but he did not know the mania of her eagerness. She stumbled from the car with a rush and welded herself to him from chin to ankle—soft, clinging with savage insistence, burning his skin with subtle yet power-laden sorcery that demanded everything he had to give. He took no account of the fact that bits of metal on the car were cruelly gouging his back in rhythm to her pressing efforts as she crushed against him and drove him to cooperation against his initial intention. A primeval madness welled through the exultant sounds of suc-cess that came from her throat—sounds of stark brutal effort, sounds of raw exultant victory that mounted to frenzy…and then fell into lax swooning subsidence, Nature seeking the sweet lull before the final crashing storm of release. Dick felt his skin prickle as rivulets of sweat trickled down his flanks, but whether it was his, hers, or a combination of both, he could not tell.

Suddenly the metal prodding his back cut sharply into his consciousness and he moved to ease the pain, but she clutched him tighter and would not let him leave the spot. He shifted, trying to at least improve his position, and was able to breathe more freely and with less discomfort. Again he moved and again she forestalled him.

In a low, caressing voice he explained that the car was hurting him—that they would have to move to a new place. With a reluctant sigh, she began to release her hold on him but, with a hurried little gasp, clung again, and his senses reeled anew at the sensation of her skidding on his sweat-slick chest.

Taking a deep breath, he forcibly pushed her away hard and wrenched open the car door, grasping the thick maroon robe that he had seen earlier in the back seat.

The robe kept the grass stubble from cutting their skin and provided a mattress that was comfortable and relaxing after their furious ordeal. She clung to him, her lips searching his skin and biting him occasionally, while he massaged the cleft of her strong back and held her close ... ever closer.

Dawn was a smudged gray promise on the eastern horizon when he took her home. They parked the car at the garage and walked quietly so as not to awaken her parents, although Annette loftily announced that she was her own boss.

"Your dad is my boss," he reminded her.

"What about me?"

"You have your points," he told her casually.

She stopped at the front gate and faced him. "Dick, don't you love me?"

"Sure. Just as much as you love me."

"I don't like the way you said that."

He shrugged. "My women like me as I am. You're just all overcome with this night. You don't love me."

"That's not true," she flared hotly. "I'd never ... never ... well, if I hadn't loved you."

"That happened afterward, my dear. Let's not get confused about it. At the party you didn't like me for two cents. It was only after we stopped in the car that you suddenly found that you loved me. Examine that kind of love and see if it's what you want for the rest of your life."

"If it's good enough for Janey, it's good enough for me."

Scathingly he was impelled to cut her down and he saw a subtle way of doing it.

"I think there'll be sufficient for both of you."

With those parting words, he left her standing on the sidewalk, her face flaming with suppressed rage, rage that rang from her staccato footsteps and the crash of the gate as she slammed it behind her.

Before Dick was fifty feet away from the Peters' residence, he suddenly and unaccountably became aware of a new thought clamoring into his mind—the image of Karel Snowden as she stood beside the old antique desk in Fannie Blumendahl's study. The sweep of her soft hair, the flawless skin of her neck, the foothills of her proud young breasts swelling over the neck of her dress, the depth of her cool green eyes and the slight touch of sadness to her lips. The picture that he had retained was so vivid that it staggered him for a moment. He shook his head. Dr. Franchette, by insisting that he meet her, had set up an immediate resistance within him and the meeting he had faced as a chore, something to go through with mechanically, then forget. His subconscious mind had retained a shockingly clear picture of the girl, then thrust it into his consciousness when he least expected it. He went to bed reluctantly thinking of her, went to sleep with her enigmatic eyes searching his soul. She had pierced his hidden recesses, stripping away the curtain and leaving him naked and somewhat chilled. The whole thing grew to monstrous proportions in his mind as he tossed and turned restlessly in his bed.

"Damn her," he muttered resentfully. "Damn her and her green eyes. She's no better—no different—than the rest of 'em." But something within him told him he was wrong, deeply wrong, and with the feeling of a shipwrecked man clutching at a straw, he knew he would have to find out for himself—no matter what it might cost him.

CHAPTER SEVEN

MOHAMMED tossed his shapely head and pawed the ground with feet that looked like those of an equine dancer. Mohammed was an Arabian stallion, the pride and joy of Fahenstock and the bane of the stable boy's existence. He was tall, as slim as a racer, trimmed like a clipper ship and full to his soft black eyes of pure fiery hell and sudden, explosive action. He was not a mean horse but a horse accustomed to having his own way. That day in the paddock out in back of the big barn, he faced Elk with the arrogant stare of a king who would brook no trifling. Elk was tall and skinny and fearful of the horse.

He approached him warily, a bridle held outstretched in a manner that he hoped was enticing, but Mohammed danced in a circle, keeping his head toward the stable boy, his pink nostrils flaring and his long white mane and tail whipping ominously in the breeze.

"Come on, boy…come on, boy. Miss Fannie say I got to exercise you…come, boy, come boy."

The stallion whistled a challenge, wheeled away only to turn and race furiously at the colored boy, whirling and delivering a terrific kick with both hind feet. As he wheeled to see why they hadn't connected, a spurt of fire lashed him from withers to flank, a loud report accompanying the skin-crawling pain. With a snort of terror he wheeled to see the slim figure of a girl standing within ten feet of him.

"Look out, Miss Karel—that horse is dangerous!" yelled Elk.

"He's not dangerous," she said calmly. "He's just nervous and inclined to be brash. Give me the bridle."

He handed her the bridle with a groan. "Lawd, Lawd, ef that hoss jump on you, Miss Fannie gonna skin me."

"He's not going to jump on anyone. You go stand near the gate, Elk. I don't think he likes you."

"I don't think it," muttered Elk with conviction. "I *knows* it." He moved toward the gate, put his back against it and watched the proceedings. Slowly Karel dropped the whip in plain sight of the horse and approached him with deliberate steps. "Be still, boy," she said in a calm voice. The voice had strength in it, command, and seemed to soothe him. He tossed his head and sent a shuddering question from his nostrils. "It's all right, son ... take it easy." Her hands caught his forelock, patted their way down his neck and stroked his glassily smooth shoulder. He let out a gusty sigh of relief and docilely allowed her to put the bridle on him. Like a great white dog, he tagged along behind her as she lead him out of the gate that Elk, his eyes wide with wonder, opened for them.

"You sure put the hoodoo on him," he declared. "Ain't nobody can ketch him like that."

"I did," said Karel. "What were you going to do with him?"

Elk rubbed his nose with his wrist. "I was goin' to try to ride 'im—that's what Miss Fannie say. Look like all he need is to be turned loose. Then he can run all he wants to."

"I'll ride him. Where's the saddle."

"Whichun, the stock saddle or the English one?"

"I'll take the stock saddle. That little bun of an English saddle is too much like riding bareback."

"That's what I say, too. Bring 'im on in. I got it strung up by the pummel. You put the blanket on 'im and I'll let the saddle down. Reckon he'll let me girt it up?"

"I'll do that. You just let the saddle down and be careful that you don't let it fall and scare him."

Elk edged around behind the horse and untied the rope, holding up the saddle.

Fannie was sitting on the front verandah sucking on a highly satisfying highball that Lula had fixed for her—and content and at peace with all things—until the horse came into her vision, cantering in his peculiar, high-backed, side-stepping way that showed restraint being forced upon him.

The girl gave him his head for a moment and he stretched out in a furious run, his nostrils fluttering from boisterous snorts of eagerness. Fannie leaped to her feet with a bellow that made Lula back hastily away from the liquor cabinet at the back of the house and wipe her mouth guiltily. "Hey, you idiot ... Karel! Get off that man-killing demon this instant ... do you hear me?"

Karel, hearing the strident yell, looked, waved and turned the horse toward the house. Across the smooth pasture he raced, a horse-lover's dream of flying hoofs and smoothly rolling muscles, his clear white hide glistening in the sun and his luxurious tail streaming out behind him.

Karel let him run almost to the verandah before pulling him to a sliding stop in which he immediately reared and fought the air with his forefeet. Fannie paled and made a stricken sound deep in her throat as the girl pulled up her whip and dealt him a smart blow between the ears. He subsided with a whoosh and stood trembling with eagerness for more frolic. Fannie sat heavily in her chair, slowly regaining some of her color.

"Whatever possessed you to pull such a stunt as that?" she stage-whispered, fearing to talk aloud lest Mohammed rear again.

"Why, he's a darling. We understand each other perfectly, don't we, boy?" Mohammed seemed to and nodded his head vigorously. "See, he heard me."

Fannie gripped her hands until the palms sweated. "Don't you know that horse is a killer? He put Elk's father in that wheel chair. He'll never walk again."

Karel shrugged her lovely shoulders and stood nonchalantly in the stirrups to allow Mohammed to pluck a tuft of grass. "They don't know how to handle him. You saw how obedient he is to me. I'm going to take him out into the back pasture and ride him until he foams like laundry soap."

Fannie waved her away. "All right. Ride him if you must, but get out of my sight or I'll have a litter of purple unicorns. It unnerves me. I don't care how well you handle him—it unnerves me."

Dick, having caught up with his work, found himself bored and unoccupied. It was early afternoon, and lunch at Mrs. Pinkney's was always a meal of such delight and proportions that, as usual, he had overeaten and was now logy, hot and sticky with sweat.

Jeff Peters came in, mopping his thick neck and puffing. "Hot."

"Sure is."

"Finish them statements?"

"Yes, sir. Was that all of them?"

"Yeah—all that go out this time. Why don't you go somewhere and swim or something? No need for you to stay around here and get steam-struck. I'll lock up."

Dick accepted the offer with alacrity, and within twenty minutes he was racing his car toward a stream he had seen the night he had gone to Fannie's party. The road took him through a tunnel of leafy green, cool and peaceful, and ended abruptly at a deep declivity shaded by great oaks and magnolias—a cool, sweet dungeon of quiet, broken only by the sawing of cicadas and crickets. He got out of the car and approached the stream, giving tongue to an exclamation of pleased surprise. A deep round pool was there, shaded by the trees and the high bank. Obviously it had been used by others before him because there was a diving board of sorts, a frayed rope tied to a high branch where boys had swung out to splash in the clear water, and the bank was worn smooth of grass by the passage of bare feet. He stripped to the buff in a matter of seconds, took a running start and sprang high from the board, entering the water like a spear. Down, down he went, the cold shock chasing away the day's accumulated heat and making his muscles contract. When the pressure began to pound in his ears, he shot upward to the surface and rolled and splashed in an orgy of sensual abandonment. Tiring momentarily, he swam to the opposite shore and lay in the damp sand, savoring its coolness. He relaxed gradually and after a time fell into a quiet, dreamless sleep. An hour later he awoke refreshed and eager for another swim, but sounds came to his ears that stopped him—a horse's hoofs thundering against hard, dry earth. They faded and disappeared only to return gradually and reach a crescendo at a spot not too far from the creek. Then they faded again. Curious, he crawled up the creek bank and walked through the grassless woods until he came to an opening that revealed what he took to be about a thousand acres of rolling meadow land.

Again the sound of the racing horse came to his ear. Hiding himself so he could peer over a thick bush, he waited until the horse and rider came into view. His eyes widened at the sight of the girl urging the cavorting horse to efforts that seemed to make him skim the ground like a swallow. "Arabian," he whispered with awe. "Ye gods, what a horse." After more passes up and down the pasture, they whirled about and headed straight for his hiding place. Dick cursed and crouched low in his leafy retreat, hoping that she would pass him by and wondering if by some freak of vision she had seen his head projecting above the bush. She rode the horse into the shade, and by this time he could tell that the girl was Karel. The realization was accompanied by such a mental and physical shock that he was outraged and angry at himself. Unreasonably, he was even a little angry at her for no cause that he could identify. In jodhpurs, high-heeled western boots and scarlet skirt, she seemed very young, fresh and sweet in a way that hurt his breast, making him even angrier at himself—an anger that confused and annoyed him.

The white horse cropped grass while the girl walked about, plucking grass blades and making squawkers of them, sitting with her back to the trunk of a tree and talking in a low, melodic voice to the horse, who pricked up his ears and stopped grazing to listen to her.

Dick's position became excruciatingly cramped, necessitating a change. If he changed position, the horse might hear him, so moving might also mean precipitous retreat but he chanced it, creeping until he was a hundred feet away and then sprinting at top speed toward the creek. The water that had previously thrilled and calmed him now irritated him beyond endurance and he swam across, an angry scowl furrowed into his forehead. He put on his clothes quickly, started his car and left the vicinity with enough speed to break a spring—he wondered as he pulled up on the main road how he hadn't.

The afternoon seemed suddenly doomed to failure. His mind was troubled and so filled with the Mona Lisa face of the girl that he could not dispel his aching resentment toward her and, worse, toward himself. What was there about her that made him feel so lowly, so unworthy? His cheek, which had been well for some days, started paining and so it was a short-tempered Dick that stalked into Abe Mullins' bar and demanded a bourbon four times tall.

"Looks like you're a mite put out about sumpin'," said Abe as he poured the drink. "Sort of a mickey slug fer a beer drinker."

"I've been here once before. I drank a beer. That doesn't make me a beer drinker."

"No, I reckon not," answered Abe equably. "No skin offa my nose. You order 'em and I'll serve 'em."

"Good," said Dick as he gulped half the drink and sipped water behind it.

"Looks like you always hit it wrong," said Abe.

"Why?"

"Here comes Mr. Jack and he ain't in a good humor either."

"Two-to-one I'm in a worse humor than he is."

"A bet," said Abe, locating the bungstarter and leaning back with crossed arms.

Jack McGrew came in, his lips hanging loosely, his brooding and bloodshot eyes wandering around the dimly lighted bar until they saw Abe, narrowed and traveled on to Dick. His thick fists clenched.

"Ah-h-h." His breath went out and he stepped toward Dick. "I've been looking for you, Mr. Son-of-a-bitch." The earlier scene repeated itself, with two sharp cracks ringing through the air and then the dull crash as the big man fell to the floor.

"This," said Dick, blowing on his smarting knuckles, "is getting monotonous."

Abe grinned and peered over the bar. "Better look and see if he ain't got a beer bottle in his pocket. I ain't never figgered out where that other'n come from."

Jack sat up and fingered his jaw, which was beginning to swell.

"You ain't havin' too good luck," said Abe amiably. "Why doncha go on home and sleep it off?"

The other pointed a trembling forefinger at him. "You hit me the other day," he brayed accusingly.

"Sure did. Aim to do it again if you start any killin's in here. I don't go fer throwin' bottles, kickin' a man when he's down and such. What'f he'd a-took his feet to you either time? You was out long enough fer him t' stomp the guts out of you."

"I'll take my business elsewhere," McGrew said with offended dignity.

"I'd sleep better if I could depend on it."

With startling suddenness Jack climbed to his feet and brought a battered brass spittoon with him which he hurled at

Dick with all his strength. Again, caught by surprise, Dick was not quick enough to dodge the missile and it took him full in the stomach. Jack missed his aim because of his poor grip and the speed with which he had thrown it. Dick crumpled forward, catching a right swing in the stomach, and the left missing his jaw and almost throwing McGrew off balance.

Abe did not have to leap the bar this time because the melee occurred within his reaching distance. He drew back, struck, pulled a tuft of hair from his mallet and stowed it carefully away before going around the bar and ministering to the prone men.

Dr. Franchette's sensitive fingers explored Dick's abdomen for a few seconds. "How does it feel?"

"Sore."

"To be expected. How did he miss your head this time?"

Dick's grin was wan but spontaneous. "I don't know. The man's a magician. I've been underestimating him, too. I won't do that again, you can bet."

"Very well. You may get up and dress."

Dick dressed quickly and accepted a drink from Maude in the Doctor's study.

"I've been meaning to ask you, Doctor. What about this girl who lives with Mrs. Blumendahl?"

Dr. Franchette felt a little thrill. "What about her?"

"Who is she? What is she to you?"

"Well, you could call her a joint ward of Fannie's and mine. We are sponsoring her, in a manner of speaking. Why do you ask?"

"I was wondering if there'd be any objection to my seeing her?"

"I shouldn't think so—except for one thing."

Dick raised his head quickly. "What is that?"

Dr. Franchette leaned forward, his face serious. "Son, I wouldn't want to hurt your feelings, but if you recall, your attitude toward women, as you outlined it to me, is hardly one conducive to agreement on our part."

The bullish cast came to Dick's face and his jaws grew hard. "Oh, yes, I had forgotten. Please forgive me."

"Of course," said the Doctor affably. "Nothing ventured, nothing gained."

Dick walked home afflicted with a strange malady. He was sick with a kind of sickness he'd never had before—the leaden nausea that is produced when one is faced with the fact that one is not acceptable as an escort for a lovely girl. In his position he stood impaled upon the horn of his own making, self-convicted of an attitude unacceptable to Dr. Franchette and most assuredly unacceptable to that old grenadier of a woman with whom the girl stayed.

"Crucified, by God …" he burst out verbally against the rotten turn of fate that had made him perform so stupidly and, unable to face the thought of his lonely, dim room at Mrs. Pinkney's, he turned toward town and ended up in Abe Mullins' bar.

"Well, you come back a lot quicker this time," Abe observed.

He nodded and took the last stool. The others were occupied by men whom he did not know and didn't care to meet. "Set me up a foredecker again, Abe. I crave oblivion."

Abe grinned. "I got a bungstarter here that's a lot faster."

"Thanks, I'll take it the easy way… and thanks for both times. I guess you saved me from being disfigured for life."

"That ain't why I done it," said Abe, wheezing out a short laugh. "You like to bet and you ain't very good with the horses."

"That reminds me," Dick grinned fleetingly, "I owe you another ten spot."

Abe took the bill from the counter and put it in his pocket.

"That's what I was hoping it would remind you of… nope, that drink is on me and the next one, too. I'm way ahead of you."

Three fourdeckers later Dick felt no pain of any sort and could even control the parade of images in his mind. Feeling very

fit and equal to mighty performances, he started home regret-
fully. A feeling like this certainly did not deserve to be put to bed
and so he turned into the Blue Plate Café and called Janey. She
was home, she was alone and she would like nothing better than
to build him a drink. Feeling even more exuberant, he stepped
off down the street like a soldier on parade.

Janey led him to a couch and eyed him solemnly while he sat
down. "I don't know whether I like you or not."

"Me?—How come?"

"I heard that you took Annette to Fannie Blumendahl's
party."

"Well, let's say she took me. My car was on the blink."

"Never mind the details." She sat beside him, her face sag-
ging with woe.

"Dick, why will you do me that way?"

"Oh, hell…" He sat up straight and glared at her. "You two
women give me a pain where I sit. You play games all your life,
then as soon as the table turns on you, you get all saddened and
feel that the world's turned against you. Games…remember?
Well, I wanted to see who played the best."

She sighed dolefully. "Who did?"

He cackled with glee. "Now wouldn't you like to know that?
A smart girl could figure it out. I go out with you. I go out with
Annette. The next one I see is you. Simple mathematics."

She bounced up, mollified, and ran back into the dining
room to get drinks. Dick's eyes were sour as they watched her
depart. "Fool," he muttered. "Melt you both together and all
you'd be is high-grade stall-fed beef with twitches in the right
spots at the right time. Not a decent trick or spot of strategy.
You're thick, both of you, and I can see through you like well
water. Transparent…" This stopped him. The last time he had
heard that word he had been slugged between the eyes with
it. Tonight, under almost identical circumstances, he had
been slugged again. With fluid ease he skidded the unpleasant

thought from his consciousness and thought only of the business at hand.

Janey returned with the drinks, and she had changed to a short Chinese coat embroidered with golden dragons on silver-blue silk. It struck her just above the knees, and, from the way her body slipped beneath it, he knew it was all she wore.

"Put the drinks down and come here," he said thickly. "We can drink later."

She was warm and palpitant in his arms, and her mouth was a sweet cave that tried to engulf him. The touch of her firm flesh beneath his hands sent a splintering shock of sensation over him, driving out all other thought in finding that his own intentions were being reinforced with zeal and fervency. All things ceased to be save that moment, that place and an object that preceded man into the world. It seemed that the dragon came alive, its scaly tentacles changing to strong columns of ineffable muscular smoothness that gripped him with that undeniable power seeking release from the most primitive urge on earth.

The surf beat thunderously in his ears and a tumult rocketed through him until he seemed to fall through space, strangling, suffocating. He knew it was the suffocating. He knew it was the smother of her hair coming loose and cascading over his face with a thick veil of softness.

CHAPTER EIGHT

IF DICK considered that his ill-advised remark to Dr. Franchette concerning women placed him in an unfavorable position, the day after the Doctor's smiling rebuff found him in one considerably worse. He sat before his desk checking a long list of figures and was astounded to find five mistakes. He had made but one mistake since going to work for Jeff Peters and that had been when the front man put in a sale without ringing it up on the register. Five mistakes ... she rides that horse like Diana ... the way her hair flows back over her ears ... the curves of her erect but supple body. He shook his head and mopped the sweat from his face. Five mistakes ... and he'd make more if he didn't put her out of his mind and concentrate on his figures. Five mistakes ... Dick sat back and lit a cigarette, letting the checking go for a while. He thought of Janey and the night before, then he thought of Karel and the proximity in his thoughts of the two girls made him almost ill. He clenched his teeth and looked guiltily about. Was this the reaction of a hard man, an opportunist, who had deliberately set about to take all from as many women as possible and give nothing in return? A feeling of sweet, suffocating resentment swelled in his chest and anger furrowed his brow. He was Phillip Richard Gamble and that was that. The girl was probably as dumb as a knot, uninteresting and a complete hayseed. With this starveling bit of comfort, he dashed through the figures again, with no mistakes—but there she was, her image forming against the wall before him in such etched detail that he sat back for a moment and gave himself up completely to the delightful job of studying her closely.

"Dick, how's about walking down to the Post Office and bringing the mail back? Annette forgot it or took it home, I don't know which."

"Okay, Jeff. I might stop at the Café and get a Coke. This is going to be another hot day."

"Take your time." Jeff waddled back to his office, mopping his neck and head.

Coming out of the Post Office with an armful of circulars but no important mail, Dick had to move aside to avoid Fannie Blumendahl, who strode on past him with a stiff nod. His searching glance soon picked up the buckboard and Morgans under the old oak tree three doors down and in it sat Karel, dressed in Levis, boots and a white shirt. Her hair was pulled back and tied with a pale blue ribbon, making her look almost childish. Dick swallowed hard and started toward Main Street, only to stop again and look back at the girl. He stuffed the mail in his pockets and strode belligerently toward the buckboard.

"I'm Dick Gamble," he said almost truculently as he reached the side of the horses and patted one of them absently on a hip. "I met you the other night at the party."

Karel's expression changed only in that a faint smile touched her lips. "Yes, I remember. How do you do?"

"Very well, thank you. I, er … I'm glad to see you."

Her eyebrows went up infinitesimally and Dick felt like a fool. "You are? I had the impression the other night that you were bored to death. You certainly didn't stay around long."

"Well … that is, I didn't feel so good at the time."

"Oh, you were tight?"

"No, it wasn't that. It …" He floundered and stopped, unable to meet the cool eyes that had him fastened tightly.

"What was it?" she prompted gently, inexorably.

Dick began to feel the fingers of panic tickle his spine. This girl had a flair for making him uncomfortable and her blunt conversation left him little protection.

"As a matter of fact, I wasn't interested. Dr. Franchette told me he had someone he wanted me to meet, and you know how those things usually turn out."

"No. How do they turn out?"

Dick grasped a wheel firmly. "I was afraid," he continued, striving to meet her bluntness in like fashion, "that you'd turn out to be some dowdy, stringy-haired, bucktoothed flop and there I'd be."

A little gurgle of laughter tumbled from her lips. "I must be just that, the way you left."

He flushed. "No … not that. I went in with my mind made up and it was a day later before I realized I had been wrong." Wrong. This whole thing was wrong. Dick had always made it a point never to concede anything because with concessions went the upper hand and one lost initiative.

"Gosh, but I must have really impressed you if it took a day for you to remember me."

Dick began to get angry. "I'm afraid I can't explain it very well."

"I guess not. Those things are pretty hard to explain."

"I'd like to come to see you," said Dick, wholly and entirely without volition, hearing his own voice with a horror that chilled him.

The swallow-winged eyebrows went up again. "You talk like it would be something of an effort."

Taking a firm grip on his faculties, he said, "I have been told that I couldn't associate with you."

"Oh. my goodness. Who could have told you anything like that?"

"The estimable Dr. Franchette," he said sullenly.

The chill was unmistakable. It reached out and numbed his extremities and sent a lump of cold fear into his throat.

"Dr. Franchette told you that?"

"Y-yes he did … that is, yes." He bit the last word off and whipped his anger into being again.

"Then he had an excellent reason, Mr. Gamble. Dr. Franchette is one man who does not act without the very best reasons. Mrs. Blumendahl is coming. Good afternoon."

Dick stumbled away, almost being run down by a teenager on a racing horse, and continued over to the Courthouse green where he stood beneath the branches of a magnolia for a few minutes, trying to force his mind into order. Never in his life had he endured such an arctic atmosphere. Never had he seen one produced so swiftly or with such devastating momentum. He lifted trembling hands and surveyed them as though they did not belong to him but to an utter stranger. He shook his head and moved off toward the barroom. He never got back to work that afternoon and at dusk Abe Mullins called the Ford Place. "Hey, Jeff, better come down here and get your man. He's stuccoed."

"Who—Dick?"

"That's him."

Jeff Peters uttered an unbelieving curse and hung up. Two hours later, after driving Dick around in the cool afternoon air, Jeff pulled off the road where a tiny spring creek had made a deep pool and, pulling the limp form from the car, shoved him into the cold water. The shock brought him out of his coma, but so slowly that Jeff, cursing his own precipitousness, had to wade in and yank him out to prevent him from drowning.

"Now set there, dammit, till you get some sense. What the hell do you mean, gettin' drunk in midday—on my time?"

Dick pulled himself laboriously from the sandy puddle and sat up shakily. For a moment he breathed heavily, shuddering to qualms of nausea that seemed to spring from his very depths. He vomited, straining so hard that he went blind, shaking with a chill that gripped him hard. For a long time he sat propped on one arm, his hair hanging over his face, his whole frame jerking with spasmodic chills. Finally he flopped over on his back and groaned.

"You…can make out…my check. Pick it up…in the morning."

"You oughtta be bored for the hollow horn," snapped Peters. "Just lay there till you git up, then I'll take you home and you can sleep it off. Come on back to work tomorrow and we'll talk about it."

Dick was too sick and weak to argue. He mustered up enough strength to climb in the car, not caring whether he wet the seat or not since Jeff apparently didn't care either.

"What you so quiet about, honey?" asked Fannie as she stopped under a shade tree to let her horses blow.

"That man…"

"What man? You mean the one you was talking to when I came back?"

"Yes."

"What about him?"

"I feel sorry for him."

"You sure put the freeze on him for someone who feels a sorrow."

"He is a little strange in a lot of ways. He wanted to come to see me but Dr. Franchette has told him he can't."

"Then Doc's got a damn good reason," she said flatly. "When Theodore shuts the gate, we should take a look."

"I told him there must be a good reason. But Fannie, he's so confused and unhappy."

"Might well be, honey, but you can't carry him."

"I'd like to know him better, though."

"Well, we'll see. Have to talk to Theodore first and see what he meant by telling him he couldn't come out."

As if in answer to their thoughts, Dr. Franchette clumped around the side of the house just as they drove up in front. He wore faded khakis, carried a long fly rod in one hand and a heavy string of bass in the other.

"Took you up on that offer to fish in your lake," he said as they climbed from the vehicle.

"Don't remember invitin' you," snarled Fannie.

"Oh, you didn't in so many words. I knew you had just let it slip your mind. I'll divide with you, provided I can get a drink. I'm bushed."

"Come on in and hand those things over to Bessie and Lula. They'll clean them. I know Maude doesn't feel like cleaning fish tonight."

"I clean my own fish," he retorted with heat.

"Nuts. I'll bet if you had to clean them you'd never eat any. Come on in. Karel and I want to know why you want to build a fence around her."

Dr. Franchette sat with his wet pants' legs carefully avoiding the cushion in the big rocker. In his hand was a tall drink and in his soul, contentment.

"Now, what's all this about, wanting to build a fence around Karel?"

"You forbid young Gamble to come out here."

"Karel, my dear, will you run off and play dolls or something? I want to give Fannie a lesson in human fundamentals. You won't need to know it for another twenty years. Your instinct will take care of you now." The girl nodded and went through the twin doors into the house.

"This is a fairly long story, Fannie, which I shall attempt to cut short."

"Yes, do. I'm in no mood to listen to stories unless they are dirty ones."

His look was pained but he went on. "In the first place, the lad is as bullheaded as his father, who was as bullheaded as *his* father, and I don't know how far back that goes in the Gamble family, but as far as I can trace it, it goes a long way. Dick, at present, is not in the right state of mind to associate with our Karel. He hasn't been through the mill. He's been hurt and can't find the proper healing formula. He's disillusioned and takes umbrage as though the bitter Fates acted according to a diabolical plan, with him as the sole object. He hasn't suffered yet and has absolutely no humility. He's bright enough and sensible in more ways than you could imagine, none of them being important enough to sneeze at. I'm glad to know he has noticed her because, unless I miss my guess, he will begin to suffer before long."

Fannie nodded and took a long pull at her drink. "And what's all the suffering going to produce?"

Franchette's expressive eyebrows went up. "Who can say? Maybe a ruined man, maybe a cringing schizoid if he fails to adjust and has to retire from reality, maybe a rum-pot whose only happiness is in a state of perpetual inebriation."

"And on the other hand ...?"

"Ah ... that's it. If I'm not wrong, he'll come out of the fire a new man, a man of purpose, of strength, and a man we wouldn't mind letting see our girl. Only time will tell."

"Well, one good thing—time is not of the essence."

"I suppose not, but there are things which might indicate that maybe too much time shouldn't go to waste."

"Like what?"

Franchette sucked his lips in, making his spade beard sprout fiercely upward. "Do you think Karel is happy here?"

Fannie glowered at him. "If you're trying to trick me into one of your famous technicality-lined booby traps, I'll fool you. All I'll say is that, in comparison to her last abode, this one is heaven."

Dr. Franchette looked disappointed. "Well, looking at it that way, I suppose you're right but ..." He leaned forward. "Fannie, that girl had to grow up very suddenly. She accepted and was forced, all on the same day. I shouldn't have to tell you what a working-over her emotional self took as a result of those two occurrences."

"All right, then. Don't tell me. I'm not a complete fool. What has that got to do with what we're talking about?"

He took a crumpled piece of paper from his pocket and handed it to her. "I picked this up on the path to the lake. It had been folded, then walked on by cattle. She lost it while riding, very likely." Fannie smoothed the paper out and read it, her big body growing taut and her eyes misty. She relaxed and handed it back. "It's pretty bad, isn't it?"

"I've seen worse—published. Listen. It might sound different when I read it."

"Aching arms that fling wide their entreating crescent trap to empty night,
Aching arms that throb in cold aloneness,
Aching arms that ever seek, grasping for who is never there,
Aching arms whose sinews in disuse grow thin and soft,
Aching arms that droop from the longing weariness of empty groping,
Aching arms all alone and with never a song nor friend save that of aching heart.
Aching heart that springs fiercely aflame each day as lids open and sleep flies,
Aching heart that beats like a light-blind moth begging an end,
Aching heart that whimpers vainly to each moment, let another's heart beat find me,
Aching heart whose task is to work even amid the claws of pain,
Aching heart that cannot see and searches blindly like an infant for a breast,
Aching heart all alone with never a song nor friend save that of aching arms.
Both in their pain and distress asking why … why … why …?"

Fannie was quiet for a long time. She cleared her throat, played with her cigarette holder and then looked belligerently at Theodore. "Kid stuff … adolescent aches and pains. Aching arms—phooey."

Dr. Franchette beat dust from his shirt in an angry effort to find a cheroot. "This," he rapped out, "is the first time I ever saw you sneer at an exhibition of raw humanity. So it's bad poetry—what should it be, like Tennyson? Or some of these benighted asses who write like Picasso paints...no one knowing what the hell they're talking about? That child painted her soul on paper in a moment of acute despondency. It is raw, it is emotional truth, and it is Karel. To me it is infinitely better than any of this puke that falls out of a Greenwich Village attic window and has been worked over for three years by some hebephrenic goat with complicating avitaminosis."

"If you're trying to give me a culture complex," Fannie said harshly, "you'll fail dismally. Maybe I geel guilty about it—maybe it's even poetic history in the making. Since when did you get so riled up about a piece of maudlin poetry?"

He sighed and took a drink. "The thing is, I'm trying to show you that no matter what an improvement this home is over her former life, she can and does have spells of unhappiness. What difference does it make whether the poetry is Poe or punk? My point is proved and the fact stands. I still say that she'll find times of unhappiness because she has been exposed, fed hors d'ouvres, and now her nature is beginning to demand a full meal. It is merely an animal reaction that is beginning to have emotional repercussions, if you'll pardon the use of the words."

"All right then," agreed Fannie. "Shall we let the boy see her now—even if he's still wetting his emotional diapers?"

The spade beard danced in silence for a moment. "As a matter of fact, I think we will...once. Something of a revealing nature might happen. After that we will decide or let Karel decide for us. I do not sell that girl's intelligence short, no matter what her nature demands."

Fannie chuckled. "You should have seen her put the freeze on him today when he told her you had forbidden him to see her.

She sent him packing and he looked like someone had slapped him in the face with a sack of cold chicken guts."

"Do you have to be crude?"

"If I so desire, you're damn right I do. You have no idea how much my crudeness and cussin' relieves me. Now that it's settled, let me go back to that poem or, rather, to poems. Why is it that those things you speak of as Greenwich Village garbage get such rave notices and people profess to just love the hell out of them?"

Franchette sighed. "It springs from the same thing that militant and truculent labor movements spring from. Incompetents always use smokescreen methods to hide behind because they are unwilling or unable to compete, as standards stand. Publishers and their stooges, the critics, go gaga over some drivel from a paraplegic mind and spend a few million 'educating' the public, which is slobbering to be in on the latest thing so as to intimidate their neighbors with their culture. In all matters of art, if those at the bottom can't compete with those at the top, they evolve some brand of abstruse crap that the men at the top wouldn't touch with a ten-foot pole. Art was once the reproduction of definite things with, of course, its ultimate triumph, the painting of beautiful women—creation's greatest achievement. Now it has all been changed. A painting is raved over if it has a leg, an arm, a breast and three or four lidless eyes scattered about. Why? What was it drawn from, what does it represent? The artist's conception of some integrated thing, a magnificent human being? Then he must be a raving maniac and should be locked up. The whole fabric of the arts today is smeared by the have-nots claiming that the haves are crass commercialists, mere draughtsmen—anything but artists. Were it not for the fact that this queer herd has taken vast liberties with Webster to prove that what they do is art and anything else is only a substitute, there'd be none of this psychotic stuff loaded on a gullible public in the name of art.

These half-baked aesthetes would have to call it something else, which might discommode them for a second, but esoteric jargon is their stock-in-trade."

Fannie leaned back and roared with laughter. "By God, but I love to get you strung out on something like that—. Now give me a treatise on what morals are and what they should…or shouldn't…be."

"I'm dry," he said with a grin, "and I refuse to be badgered into something that always makes me sore. When shall we let the boy see her?"

"That's a problem, if he's as hardheaded as you say. Suppose we just let him stew for a little while longer."

Dick could be depended upon to stew. The next morning he stewed in agony resulting from the previous night's debauchery, anguished both in psyche and in soma. The soma clamored for attention, due in part to his having passed up his breakfast but due principally to the amount of whiskey that he had loaded into it. Pale and sallow-green, he sat limply at his desk and gave himself over to a grueling attack of the shuddering mutters. Jeff entered and surveyed him with kindly eyes.

"First time you was ever that drunk, huh, Dick?"

Dick, too ill to speak, nodded.

"What did you have for breakfast?"

His only answer was a reproachful look.

"Unh hunh. That's what I thought and that's where you made your mistake. Couldn't git much sicker could you?" Another shake of the head.

"Okay. I'm gonna fix you up and if you don't take it, I'm gonna drown you in it." Jeff left and returned in five minutes with a quart cup of warm soda water. "Here, take this stuff to the toilet and drink it. Hold it as long as you can, then let it go. When you get done, I'll have somethin' else for you."

Dick stood over the toilet, hostilely eyeing the cup of warm water. Soda…warm…Jesus! Gritting his teeth with resolution, he raised it to his lips and emptied it in one long pour. He reeled against the wall and strove mightily to hold it, but after a few minutes it returned with a rush. In two innard-tearing efforts he cleared his stomach and turned away, dripping with sweat, and walked back to his office. Jeff came in ten minutes later with something in a paper bag.

"How'd it go?"

"It went," mumbled Dick shakily. "Then it came back. I feel a little better though."

Jeff pulled a quart of milk from the bag. "Here, now, Drink this, every damn bit, even if it takes all morning." He poured out a paper cupful and handed it across the desk. Dick tasted the cold fluid with care. Then, as its chilling balm struck his empty stomach, he drank thirstily.

"Hold it—not so damn fast. Take it easy and it'll stay put," Jeff cautioned.

It stayed put and by eleven o'clock Dick was feeling well enough in body to become thoroughly ill in mind, and between the two, the former condition, now that it had abated, seemed immeasurably preferable. Constantly before his eyes was the image of the girl's face, the kind warmth of her eyes that had so suddenly changed to spheres of green ice, the soft appeal of her voice that had instantly frozen into cold and distant tones of rejection.

After work he went to his room and lay across the bed, weary in body and tortured in mind. That his predicament was directly due to his own eagerness to appear the hard guy, to appear immune to the attraction of women except for one thing, occurred to him, but it was a truth of such ego-bruising brutality that he shoved it aside. In addition to his immediate suffering was the gradually growing and painful realization that a great many of his conflicts were rooted in fear—an overwhelming fear of failure. He had dodged his way through life, always managing to avoid any real tests of his true inner stamina.

He had loved medicine but when his father had suggested it, he had rebelled. Rebellion! That one word was the crux of his whole existence, the fuel that fired his every thought and action. He sat up in bed seized by the idea. Me—I've done it to myself—most of it. Not all though—there were other things not all my fault. But always trying to get out from under, that's me. All right, so what? What do I do now? Crawl, make up for it, admit where I've been wrong and try to make up the difference? Be big? How? How does a person go about being big. What is bigness? Lack of confidence? Lack of drive? Lack of conviction? Giving up the ship because the going is hard? Rationalization, purely. Trying to argue with yourself again. You'll never get anywhere like that. Why can't you be honest? What's the first step—admitting that this girl has you where you've never been had before? Dick groaned as if in physical pain. What should he do? Go to that damned old Doctor with the x-ray eyes and eat crow, plead? He shuddered. The very core of his being was revolted at the idea.

With his mind whirling, he reached for the easiest solution—the few drinks that would, he told himself, help him to think straight. He got up and put on his shoes.

Abe raised his eyes in disbelief. "Nope—must be your twin brother. I didn't think you could stand even the smell today."

"I'm a man of unsuspected talents," said Dick with forced gaiety as he sat on a stool. "A four-timer."

Abe chuckled as he poured the drink. "You ain't got no talent for drinkin'. I seen that yesterday."

"What do you mean? I must have drank a fifth."

"You drank exactly two jiggers over a pint. I drink that much fer breakfast every mornin'."

Dick mulled. So you've been telling yourself that you really put it away. Just like you. Dress everything up in your favor and pretend that anything else is a lie. True to form. He shook his head and downed the drink, but the voice of his newly born other self did not leave. It stayed on even after he had consumed enough liquor that Abe put the lock on the bottle.

"That's half a pint, bub. Not another drink fer you."

"You mean you refuse to sell me another drink?"

"That's what I mean."

"I'll take my business somewhere else."

"Sound just like Mr. Jack, but you ain't gettin' another'n here. Gotta look out fer youngsters like you."

Dick staggered beneath a landslide of contrition. This man was trying to do him a favor, had probably saved his life twice, and he was about to become angry with him. "Sorry, Abe. I must still be crazy."

"Not no more'n usual fer a lad your age. Beats all how they ever git grown."

"I think I know what you mean. Better call Dr. Franchette. I see Jack McGrew coming."

"That silly bastard must watch you and foller you here. Think you can take him on?"

"Hell, yes. I won't bet tonight, though. I'm through with betting and losing."

Jack McGrew stepped into the bar and walked over to Dick, stopping at a safe distance.

"Gamble, are you prepared to marry Janey Hardwicke?"

"What the hell are you talking about?"

"I asked you a question."

"How'd you like a bust in the kisser?"

"I didn't come here to fight. I just came to ask the question."

"The answer then, my boy, is no."

"You'd better reconsider."

Dick slid slowly off the bar stool, his feet solidly apart and his arms swinging low and freely. "Beat it, putty face."

McGrew looked at him for a moment, then turned on his heel and walked out.

"What do you make of that, Abe?"

"Dunno. Ever git rapid with 'er?"

"Ummm. I don't ever talk about things like that."

"Damn fine of you, too, bub. Most men talk too goddam much. She let him take her home from the Post Office yesterday, if that means anything."

"Well, if you won't sell me any more whiskey, I guess I'll go home."

"Here's a short one on the house. Go on home and git some sleep that ain't next door to death."

"You talk like you know how it is."

"I was drunk onct."

If Dick had once thought Janey was a forward wench, he was certain of it when he turned on the light in his room and found her in his bed with the cover pulled up around her neck. She motioned for silence and whispered, "I came in through the French doors and just hoped no one but you would come in."

She had fitted the sheet to herself like molded rubber and the outline, with the twin peaks of her breasts, her slim waist and smoothly swelling hips and thighs, set his pulses to hammering. He turned out the lights.

It was an hour later and they lay in each other's arms, close, hot with recently expended passion and the fury to which it had driven them.

"Love me, Dick?"

"No."

"Why?"

"That's a stupid question."

"Why?"

He didn't answer but pulled away from her.

"I think this is all you like me for," she accused.

"This isn't enough?"

"Not for Janey, it isn't."

"What does Janey want—my heart, lungs, liver and lights?"

"You're being flip and nasty."

"Oh, Jesus. Why don't you go home?"

She hurled the cover from her and leaped to the floor. "All right, Mr. Hard Guy. I'll go home and don't you come calling me up when you can't find Annette."

"I won't," he promised. "I can usually find her."

She made a furious sound and slipped on her robe. "I hate you, Dick Gamble."

"Goody," he said, yawning widely.

She composed her face, narrowing her eyes. "You know I might be just the one to puncture that balloon of insufferable self-esteem you have so much of."

"You're getting corny. Go home."

"Do you know that Jack McGrew would kill you if I said the word?"

"Now there's the guy for you. Why don't you marry him and live happily afterward? You'd have ten squalling, snotty brats and weigh two hundred pounds in ten years."

She tied her sash with cold deliberation and, with a final long look at him, turned and went through the French doors.

"Well," he said stretching, "that is that." He could not be expected to know that it was not.

CHAPTER NINE

D R. THEODORE FRANCHETTE was indulging in two of his most popular pastimes. He was badgering his son and drinking Bradsher's Special Age with crushed ice, ginger ale and a twist of lime peel.

"And so your abdominal cramps turned out to be a perforated ulcer? Well, well. It took me a few months to learn how to diagnose them, too. What finally decided you?"

Albert sipped his drink and frowned. "No abdominal history. Rigidity at the onset but not when I examined him. Blood count out of sight, but he did have a history of a chronic appendix."

"So you went in looking for a hot appendix, found instead that a hot peritoneum upset the wall and threw things into a general mess."

"You could say that. The main point is that the man will live ... isn't it?"

Franchette cackled and wagged his beard. "We might say so, I suppose. When Christopher remarked that the advent of the sulfas and penicillin was not a free license to poor surgical technique and diagnosis, I suppose he was thinking of sprouts like you and—was that a knock?"

Maude nodded. "Dry bones, no doubt."

"I doubt it," he said, but he got up and went out on the porch. "Who's there?"

He could make out a thickset figure near the steps. "Doc, it's me, Lester."

"Lester?"

"Yes, sir. You know, from out in the fifth ward. You took that water head from my waife that time."

"Oh, of course, Lester Merrick. What can I do for you, Lester?"

"You already done enough for me, Doc. I come to do somethin' for you. You know old Rathborne?"

"Yes."

"Well, he was out to Bethlehem Church last night and he was talkin' to them Daltons after the service. 'Course, we all knows you took his granddaughter frum him, but he's done got a lawyer."

Franchette grew tense. "A lawyer? Who?"

"Plumb forgot his name. Seems like he's a sorta big shot from Baton Rouge. I heard him tell them Daltons that he was goin' to hit you in the face with a writ or court order or somethin' before long."

The Doctor frowned and gnawed his mustache. "Why are you telling me this, Lester?"

Lester squirmed and scrubbed a worn shoe against the brick wall. "Well, Doc, seein' as how I couldn't never seem to pay you nuthin', when the time come that I could turn you a favor, I done it. You done me plenty in your time."

"Well, that's very nice of you and I appreciate it a lot. In fact, you've probably saved a very lovely girl a great deal of unhappiness."

"Anything to oblige, Doc," mumbled Lester. "Well, I gotta be goin'. I rid my mule in and she ain't as rapid as she was onct. G'night."

"Good night, Lester, and thanks again." He turned slowly about and walked back into the house. On an impulse he stopped by the telephone and rang Fannie Blumendahl.

"I despise people who interrupt my after-supper highball," she bellowed, making Franchette wince.

"My ears," he complained. "I have some news I think you ought to hear that has to do with our mutual interest. Are you busy tonight?"

"I'm never busy. Come on out and why don't you bring you-know-who so we can whet the hell out of his appetite and make him suffer some more?"

"I'll be there shortly. I'll see what I can do."

He hung up and rang Mrs. Pinkney's. "Hello, Alice? This is Dr. Franchette. May I speak to your boarder, Young Gamble?"

There was a silence that lasted some five minutes before Dick's voice, thick and not too steady, came over the wire. "Yeah?"

"Dr. Franchette, Dick. I'm going out to Mrs. Blumendahl's house and I thought you might like to take the ride with me."

"Why?"

"No particular reason. I dislike riding alone at night. I might have a flat."

"If you weren't an old man, I'd call you a liar."

Franchette chuckled delightedly. "I'll pick you up in ten minutes." The sigh he heard made him wriggle with discomfort. He disliked gouging people in sensitive places.

"Better make it twenty minutes, Doc. I gotta shave and shower some of the whiskey out of my brain."

"Very well. I'll come around and gossip with Mrs. Pinkney till you get ready."

Dick was reasonably sober when he settled into the car seat beside Dr. Franchette but the clearer his mind became, the more he resented what was happening to him. "I'd like to know," he asked bitterly, "why the hell I'm letting you drag me out on this junket?"

"Maybe because you want to."

"Granted, you officious old fiend, but why? I'm in bed. I'm nearly asleep because I was drunk earlier in the evening. Then you call, and in my semi-conscious condition I allow you to drag me on this…" He made a meaningless gesture with his right hand. "I admit that the girl has attractions and I am callously turned down when I request to see her. Next thing I know, here I am on my way to her house and I want to know the reason."

"Do you believe me, Dick, when I say that were it not for the friendship I had for your father, I wouldn't bother with you for five minutes?"

"That would be the easiest thing to believe so far."

"And a long way from the truth. I see something in you that possibly you do not. I do not believe that you are what you set yourself up to be. In fact, you appear to know less about yourself than any man your age I have ever known. Because I see some worthwhile possibilities in you, I'm willing to try to help because as I see it, you slept through your formative years. Being your father's son is only a detail."

"I don't understand you at all," said Dick, making a face over a cigarette he had just lit.

"That's natural, and yet I am not a hard man to understand."

"About my sleeping, I guess you're right. I became conscious, so to speak, on a little island in the Pacific. I was washed ashore from the *Houston*—"

"And there was a woman," interrupted Franchette.

Dick turned slowly and looked intently at the little man for a long time. "You know, sometimes you frighten me and I don't like you at all. Next thing I know, I'm doing some stupid thing like this simply because you say do it. What are you trying to do? Why are you taking me with you tonight—aside from the cruelty of it?"

"Son, I'd like to have you believe that I'm trying to help you find yourself."

"But why? I'm nothing to you."

"Why do you say that?"

"Because I'm not and you know it. You just admitted that your knowing my father need not have any bearing on the matter at all."

"And there you have your answer."

Dick pondered on this for a moment. "You mean …" He flung his cigarette away. "You give me a pain in the butt, Dr. Brain-Picker Franchette."

"Interesting, picking brains." Dr. Franchette was affable. "You have no idea."

"In other words," put in Dick, "you are a meddler—a man who delights in nosing into other people's lives."

"Oh, indubitably. The people into whose affairs I have nosed are many, and let me point out a strange phenomenon. Not a single person of that number now holds it against me. Without a single exception, they are among my very best friends. I have more friends, Dick, than any one man deserves."

"That fact must carry it's own explanation," said Dick, a little angry that he had said it. In doing so, he had conceded that the old man's efforts might have been well-considered and effective. Wrong things, concessions. They put a man in a bad strategic position and give the opposition ammunition.

Franchette eyed him keenly for a second, then looked back at the road. "If you are aligning me with the opposition, you do me a rank injustice. I'm not against you. I'm for you, and time will prove what I say to be the truth."

"Look," said Dick with unnecessary heat, almost anger, "can't I have a few thoughts to myself?"

"I'm not a mind reader," said the other gently. "I've told you before, Dick, you are probably the most transparent man I know." He had done it again and Dick shriveled inwardly. What could he say, what could he think? Was he so transparent that everyone could see through him like the Doctor?

If so … He shut the thought out of his mind. At least he stayed on top of the heap when in the company of Janey and Annette. He gripped his hands until the palms sweated. Dopes, both of them. Those were the ones he could maneuver—the dopes! Then he was only a few degrees above being a dope himself. He couldn't compete with the Doctor. Neither, he suspected, could he compete with Fannie Blumendahl. Since he had lost his resentment of her suspected social intentions, he had had time to think about her more objectively and had come to fear the granite steadiness of her steel blue eyes and the truculent attitude she affected. As for Karel—he just barely stifled a groan. Here was a situation that almost choked him with gall. She had let him know in their first brief conversation that she was not only the master of her own soul but that she had possibilities of being master of his also, and the realization was a fearful blow to his vanity. To date, he had been supreme in his association with girls by the simple expedient of letting them make the first move, which invariably proved that they were interested and, therefore, cooperative. Karel was another matter entirely. This trip could be productive of nothing because he had resolved mightily not to concede another inch. If at all possible, he would recover his lost prestige but he felt pessimistic as to his chances. They seemed non-existent.

"You never had many close friends, did you, Dick?"

"No, sir. I never seemed to need them, or something..." His voice trailed off uncertainly.

"Wrong, son. Everyone needs friends and this need is not a sign of weakness. No one is totally self-sufficient in matters of the spirit or in any other way. As your friend, I could ferret out the things that are troubling you about yourself and expose them for you to see in their true light, which, you must have learned by now, is not easy for you to do yourself. It's never easy for anyone to see himself clearly because of personality defenses in which he seeks to justify his thoughts and actions rather than to analyze them. Some things are just a little more than the stomach can bear in many cases of self analysis, and it's much more pleasant to think nice things about oneself than to own up to the naked truth, which may be shockingly ugly... Now, you accuse me of picking your brain when, actually, you are an open book. I can not only make good guesses as to what is going on in your mind,

I can also predict with ninety-nine per cent accuracy how you will react, given this or that eventuality. I could have predicted your sudden propensity to hard liquor—you, essentially a beer drinker—when you were denied the privilege of seeing the girl. It follows in the pattern of everything you do, think and say. You, too, are a liar, as well as I. I lie because of deliberate intent whereas you lie because the lie is less painful than the truth. You find it either terribly hard or utterly impossible to be honest with yourself. You don't have to think back very far to realize that unless, of course, you are hopeless. If you are, you will deny what I have just said with a great deal of vigor and possibly some anger. Anger is quite revealing, as you probably understand, since you are an intelligent man."

Dick was quiet for so long that Dr. Franchette was afraid he would not speak again.

"You have me," he finally said dully, "in a spot where the more I talk, the more stupid I seem."

"Not at all. You're just beginning to wake up to a lot of well-hidden things about yourself and your motives. It takes time to come to terms with them and it takes a lot of honest effort. Stimulation through other people is of great help, so is incentive."

Dick's grin was almost painful to see. "So you supply the incentive, but I daren't touch. Is that it?"

"Not entirely. You must understand that my desire to see you recover from this state of confusion is not such that I can ignore this girl. She is very dear to me and she has endured enough from life to send many another into shrieking insanity. Instead, she has taken it in her stride, she has driven in from her mind…at least, it appears that she has. She is not one for you to practice on."

Dick almost choked from self-pity. "I will not sit here and tell you what I might or might not have done had there been no opposition to my seeing her. I will not say now what my attitude is because whatever I said would seem to have a purpose behind it."

The Doctor nodded. "When you can come to me and tell me in so many words that you were simply working off a chest full of poisonous foam when you told me about your attitude toward women, when you tell me that you have no such intentions toward Karel, then I can promise you that there will be no opposition, either from me or Fannie, to your seeing her as often as she desires. Don't forget, after you get by us, there is still the girl."

"What happens to my pride when I come crawling on my belly to you?" Dick asked, his voice trembling with bitterness.

"The same thing that should have happened to it when you were fifteen, and by that I mean the conquering of it. Pride of that sort is something few people can afford. It demands too much and produces too little. As for crawling on your stomach, haven't you ever heard of walking into a man's house with your head up and your eyes level, telling him something straight from the shoulder? In what way does that imply crawling?"

Dick put pressure on his hands until his knuckles cracked. "Either I stop seeing you, or I go crazy, or something will happen for the better. You have a certain way of hammering with logic like a blacksmith does with a sledge."

"I'm glad you see it as logic. I suspect that you are not an entirely hopeless case. I also realize that seeing something as logical and reasonable doesn't always answer all questions nor rub out all obstacles. V-day for you will be when you cease seeing the universe as a body built around a core known as Richard Gamble. You have your own particular collection of shortcomings and qualities just like the meanest man who ever walked— or the finest. Arguing with reality or bending it to excuse or justify yourself is fools' play. You'll never be totally free of error—no one ever is. But if you try to think you are you're taking the surest step toward sheer assininity—because what you think of Dick Gamble and what other people think of him are two things that will have to be brought to speaking terms. Here we are...Isn't that a magnificent old house? It makes me feel small every time I drive up to it."

Dick nodded absently, being much too occupied with thoughts of his own to be appreciative of the architectural efforts of the long dead Otto Fahenstock. His thoughts fled precipitously, however, when he realized that he would have to meet the girl presently. A cold finger probed him somewhere in the stomach and the chill sweat of fear began to dew his forehead as they walked up the ornate brick path.

Fannie sat in a tremendous rocker and waved a highball at them. "What kept you so long? I got drunk waiting."

"We drove rather slowly," said the Doctor. "You remember Dick, don't you?"

"Sure. Sit down, son. How about a drink?"

"No, thank you." He cleared his throat because his voice was quavering. "I don't think I'd better."

"What he means," said the Doctor laughing, "is that he hung a light one on earlier and doesn't care to tease it further. Where's Karel?"

"She'll be down. Dick, you may wait in the parlor if you wish. Put on some records and amuse yourself till she comes down." Dick, feeling that he was escaping from one dilemma and falling onto the horns of another, fled into the parlor with its rich velvet drapes, thick carpets, long gilt mirrors and dark mellow furniture.

Lula appeared on the verandah with a tray of drinks and when they were armed with fresh highballs, Franchette spoke. "It seems that my initial optimism was poorly founded. I have information that Rathborne is retaining a lawyer and I doubt that we can keep Karel if he goes to court. There'd be too much sentiment on his side."

"*Oh*—!" Fannie trumpeted the worst word he had ever heard her say in his life. "Now what the hell do we do? I positively will not allow that child to go back to him. I tell you I *won't*. It would kill her." She leaned forward. "Now let me tell you something once and for all, Theodore. You sat around on your dead tail and let this thing catch us like this and, by God, you can just up and figure some way out of it. Law or no law, he'll not get her and that's final." She sat back, snorting like a dragon.

He nodded meekly. "I admit fault in this case. I was too sure and too slow. We should have pinned him when we had him on the mat. It would all be over and done with now, and since there can be little doubt that he intends to take legal steps, we'd better do some fast thinking."

"It can't be too fast," she fumed. "What we want to do is to figure out something that will be final. Can't we get something on him?"

"Well, he keeps a woman over near Hammond, but somehow I detest taking any such steps because it has such a dirty smell."

"Never mind your dad-blasted sensitive nose. You do whatever needs to be done."

"Well, I mentioned it as a last resort and, of course, if we're driven, we'll have to use it. Maude knew about her, although I can't imagine how. Sometimes I think Maude is a little fey."

Dick fidgeted in the parlor. He sat down, stood up, looked at himself in one of the long mirrors, disliked what he saw and walked over to the big radio-phonograph and tried to select a program.

After discarding many records, he finally chose a number of Strauss waltzes and put them on. As the lilting strains of *Artists' Life* came softly into being, he heard a slight noise and turned just in time to see Karel come down the long, winding stairs. She had not seen him and his throat grew tight as he watched her trip lightly and rapidly down the steps. The soft white dress she wore fitted her with gentle affection, accenting her curves and caressing the full globes of her breasts. His throat grew dry and his face felt unbearably hot.

She saw him and started. "Oh…I didn't know you were here."

"Hello." His voice betrayed him again and he cleared his throat angrily.

She went across the parlor and offered him a slim hand. "I'm glad you like the waltzes. They're my favorites." He muttered something unintelligible and allowed himself to be led to a couch.

"Dr. Franchette brought you, didn't he?"

"Er…yes. How did you know?"

She did not answer but her eyes sought his with a steadiness that he found disconcerting. "I'm glad you came."

"You are? Why?"

"Because I think I was rather rude to you the other day and I wanted to apologize."

A sudden desire to save her the ignominy of an apology seized him until he realized with a start, that to her an apology would seem completely natural and honest. Ignominy was a reaction he would have, private and dishonest. "It's all right, Karel. I wasn't very nice either."

"I'm afraid you gave me a rather rough picture of the situation," she said softly, her voice churning him inside like the blades of an agitator. "I'm sorry if I hurt your feelings."

"You didn't hurt…" He stopped. That was one lie he could not tell. "My feelings are entirely too easily hurt," he added with a touch of bitterness. "They need a little beating."

"That's the hard way," she said quietly. He instantly realized that she was referring to the many times her own feelings had been brutalized. "I hope it doesn't happen that way and I don't ever want to be guilty of it."

"You're forgiven," he said with a smile, "and for my stupidity, I was properly punished."

"Oh? How?"

"Well…It doesn't matter. I was just taken down, that's all."

"And only because you wanted to see me. That's what made me feel badly."

"I still do."

She looked away for a moment before her eyes met his again. "Dick, I'm very young and I've had a lot of trouble. Fannie and Dr. Franchette have been mother and father to me. No matter what I feel, I can't go against their wills. I think I would like you. I'd like to find out anyway. Can you understand what my position is?"

He nodded, trying to swallow the hurt in his throat. "Sure, kid, I know. The whole thing is my fault and if I suffer, it's only the bed I made for myself."

"What do you mean?"

"One day, I hope, I can tell you. Right now it would sound very bad and I wouldn't want to tell you."

"You could, you know."

He searched ever line of her lovely face and knew that he could tell her, that he wanted to tell her very much, but he couldn't seem to bring it off. "Karel, you are a very lovely girl and I do think I could tell you but...I don't know. Give me a little time, will you?"

"Certainly. I didn't mean to pry."

"I don't mean that, either. You weren't prying."

"I wonder," she said with gentle affection, "if Dr. Franchette ever thinks about himself."

"Probably, but when he does, it's most likely a fleeting thing. Unless I'm wrong, he sees a problem, dissects it like he would a cadaver, examines it carefully, makes up his mind and solves everything right then and there. Then he probably forgets all about it. I used to think that people of that sort were uncomplicated but I've changed my mind. Uncomplicated people are usually dull. He certainly isn't and he is a devil in his own way."

"He's the most wonderful man in the world," she said devoutly.

"When I know him better, I'll probably agree with you."
Concession? Resolutely he thrust the thought away. He was
beginning to see things through Karel that he had seen himself
but had been unable to evaluate properly. It had caused her not
the slightest discomfort to apologize to him, and the apology was
one intended to ease the fact that she might have hurt him, not
for what she had said.

What were the emotional factors involved that she could do
this freely and not be bludgeoned by vanity? He had never been
able to bow to anything without intense suffering. Of the two
of them, he had to admit that her attitude was infinitely better
than his because she certainly had suffered no pain. She had
even seemed to welcome the opportunity to put things right. His
ego quaked somewhat as he thought of it in his usual terms of
humiliation, but then he realized that she did not prostrate herself before him either literally or figuratively. She had done what
the Doctor had suggested to him. She had told him straight from
the shoulder.

Taking a deep breath, he asked, "Then you'll let me see you?"

"As far as I'm concerned, Dick, I'll be glad to see you ... whenever they give their consent."

"Thanks," he said huskily, feeling the rise of a sensation that
angered him. Here was Dick Gamble asking favors and feeling
absurdly pleased when they were, in effect, granted ... and the
old, stubborn, sickening resentment came flooding up. He gritted his teeth and shook himself. The old Dick Gamble had never
wanted anything with this intensity—therefore, he probably
would have reacted with an indifferent shrug. Well, the new Dick
Gamble would have to do far better than that, he told himself, or
the glacial gates would surely shut in his face again, an experience he did not care to have repeated.

Suddenly, without a scrap of warning, a pain struck him in
the breast that made him gasp. In one freezing moment a light
burst upon him that made him blind and dizzy. It had never

happened before but he knew what it was—*He was in love with Karel!* Hopelessly, completely, utterly. He looked up and found her eyes studying him. Could she possibly look at him and not see it? He did not see how she could. Her eyes remained steady but the rise and fall of her breast accelerated and her hands began to maul her handkerchief. "Dick... why... why are you looking at me like that?"

"Because I can't help myself—I don't want to help myself." She lowered her eyes and a dull flush mounted to her cheek, as her breathing increased in tempo. "Karel... I didn't mean anything disrespectful. Please..." He covered her hands with his own.

Her eyes were starry when she met his anxious gaze. "I know that, Dick. I didn't mean to imply anything." Her hands turned over and grasped his. "Dick... hurry and do whatever it is you have to do." She leaped to her feet and bending, kissed him with soft, sweet insistence before she fled from the room.

For several minutes he sat still, his fingers pressed against his temples, trying to still the thunderous bedlam in his heart and brain. If she had poured scalding water on him, the astonishment would have been no greater. An involuntary sob shook him when he took a deep breath. He got up and walked out on the porch with stiff, automatic steps—the walk of a man in a state of deep shock.

CHAPTER TEN

"SO," DR. FRANCHETTE was saying, "if worse comes to worst, you and she could join Ike and Toni on some South Sea island until such time as things cleared up here. You might keep that in mind and be prepared to flee when and if I give you the call."

"You'll use that woman on him first," she said viciously. "I have no intention of leaving my comfortable house, my good cook and all I like best—except as a last resort."

"Oh, naturally, but we want to be prepared for any eventuality."

"All right, I'll be prepared for it, but I won't like it."

Dr. Franchette looked up and saw Dick standing a little distance away. "Well? She run you off?"

Dick came to earth with an effort. "Not exactly. She had some ... I mean, we ... She went to bed." His arms and legs tingled as if they were being attacked by ants and his heart still banged against his ribs with hammer blows. He sat down in a nearby rocker with such abruptness that he jarred his head, which was beginning to ache.

Franchette turned to Fannie. "Got it all through your mind now?"

"Sure, but I'm telling you, I don't want this to happen. I won't have it, so you'd better be getting a move on you."

"I'll do my best. Ready, Dick?" Dick, sunk in a deep, rosy state of semi-consciousness, did not answer. Dr. Franchette winked at Fannie. "Dick!"

The young man started and sat up. "Sir?"

"Ready?"

"Er ... yes, sir. I'm ready."

"Well, let's go."

Dick stood up and turned to Fannie. "Thanks, Mrs. Blumendahl. I ..."

"Thanks for what, son?"

"Well, I mean ... for letting me see Karel."

"Oh, that's all right. Come again ... sometime." She put a peculiar inflection to her last word that left Dick somewhat puzzled.

As they drove away, Dick fought himself into speech by main strength, physical strength that left his skin dank with sweat and the feeling that he had just finished a tough fight.

"Dr. Franchette, I'd like to talk to you again."

"No better time than now, Dick. What's on your mind?"

"Karel, sir. I'm in love with her."

"Well, you don't say? When did this happen?"

"This is going to sound silly ... just a few minutes ago."

"May I correct you?"

"Certainly?"

"It was some time ago. Maybe you just realized it tonight."

"I've got to talk." He seemed to be in a quiet frenzy. "I mean about what I told you—about my attitude and all. I guess you were right all along. I certainly couldn't think of Karel like that. I'm sorry I told you. I didn't mean it—Oh, I meant it all right but, actually, I didn't. There was too much I didn't know about, like Karel, for instance. I shudder when I think that I included her in that nasty, sweeping statement."

"Then you're hauling down your flag?"

"The pirate flag? Yes, sir. I'm flying hers from now on and I give you my word ... Jesus, that sounds stuffy ... I mean, I'll never consciously or deliberately do anything to hurt her. I mean that as much as I love life." His face was strained and white in the reflected glow of the dash light. The Doctor looked at him for a second and nodded his head.

"Yes, you mean it. You may now consider all bars down except those that Karel may see fit to raise. You have my approval and I can guarantee that of Fannie. Now, son, honestly—Don't you feel relieved, cleansed in a manner of speaking? It wasn't so bad, was it?"

"Terrible," he whispered, sinking back. "You're right, I feel wonderful now but…" He wiped his forehead with a shaking hand. "I didn't think I was going to come out with it. You'll never know what it cost me."

"I know very well what it cost you. That's what made it so hard. The next time you have to be honest with yourself it will be that much easier, and you'll always have this one to strengthen you."

Dick's buoyant step, as he walked down the sidewalk to Mrs. Pinkney's gate, was suddenly brought to a dead halt.

"I want a word with you, Gamble."

"Okay, Jack, but get it off your chest in a hurry. I don't have any time to gab with you."

"You are going to marry Janey Hardwicke."

"Oh, hell. I thought you were going to mate me with the Crown Princess of Hogovia."

"This is the last time."

"Good. You're getting on my nerves."

"I'm telling you, Gamble." Dick could feel, rather than see, the tense seriousness of the man in the darkness.

"Tell it to the Red Cross or the chaplain." He slammed the gate and walked into the house, leaving McGrew watching him with a curiously exultant look in his eyes.

Dick thought of Karel for two hours before he could go to sleep and was seized from time to time with vast, inundating waves of love, chagrin and lascivious thoughts which he strove to dispel but which came back again and again, even after he was asleep.

Although the Reverened Rathborne was listening to Mrs. McGrew with every indication of attentiveness, his mind was racing ahead of her with such speed that it was with some difficulty that he was able to talk with her.

"My dear Mrs. McGrew, believe me, I sympathize with you to the depths of my soul and you have paid me a great compliment by bringing your problem to me. Now, let me get it straight. Your son has acquired a vicious hatred for this Gamble person because of his relations with the Hardwicke girl with whom your son is enamored. That, I understand, but what can I do about it?"

Emily McGrew wiped tears from her eyes and continued. "He always admired you so. I thought maybe if you spoke to him … His father … you know . . " She made a hopeless gesture. "Frank is so short-tempered with the boy. He thinks Jack is crazy and has said so openly, even blaming me for it because of my dear father who had a nervous breakdown."

"Yes, yes, yes," said Rathborne impatiently. "Now, as I get it, you wish me to speak to Jack. Am I correct?"

"If you only would. I'm afraid he will actually do the Gamble boy some bodily harm and since Gamble is in love with your granddaughter—"

"Madam, you will please grant me the favor of not mentioning her name in my presence. No mortal should have to suffer the way I have suffered on her account."

"I'm sorry, I only meant that maybe you should speak to the Gamble boy, too. Warn him, I mean."

"Of course, of course," he muttered mechanically. "Please rest assured that I will do what I can."

When Mrs. McGrew left the house, the Reverend Rathborne sat for a long time in the dim living room, his eyes hot and feverish. Now and again he would cackle rustily and rub his dry hands together with great satisfaction. As soon as it became dark, he put on his hat and walked out of the front door, locking it carefully behind him.

Dr. Franchette had been cogitating mightily all day, and now that darkness had fallen, he sat in his study, disgruntled because he had missed a day's fishing and treating his low spirits with a highball of considerable proportions. When the rapping sounded on his door, he recognized it and cursed heartily. Not feeling at all hospitable, he called out, "Come in."

Rathborne entered the room, his hat in his hands and on his face a smirk of triumph. The Doctor snorted.

"If you've come to talk about legally turning the girl over to Fannie and me, you can turn about and leave. I'm not in the mood to discuss it. I'll contact you at my pleasure." He was deliberately baiting the other into some statement that might give light on his intended legal procedure.

Rathborne rose to the bait like an eager trout to a fly. "No," he said, taking a chair that had not been offered him. "I'm not here for that. In fact, I'm here for quite another purpose. I think it no more than fair to tell you, Theodore, that I have engaged counsel and my lawyer informs me that what you call evidence would not stand for a moment before a jury. He is even now preparing an argument that will restore Karel to her home and board."

Dr. Franchette took the announcement with calm since he had already surmised that the attack would take some such form. He sneered openly. "You were a fool to think we could have done anything in the first place. You were in a funk and we capitalized on the fact." Lead him on, infuriate him, make him talk.

Rathborne lifted his bloodless lips away from his teeth in what seemed an attempt at a smile. "You amuse me, Theodore—really you do. I allowed you to think that I was frightened in order to gain time. Time was of the essence, as they say in Spain."

"France."

"Very well. I used that time well, you will have to admit."

"I only admit to a very strong desire to throttle you, Rathborne, and before you burst from pride over your supposed coup, let me say again," he leaned forward and prodded the Minister painfully in the waistcoat, "You will never get Karel and I don't give a damn how many writs you produce or what you do. If it comes to the worst, I'll marry her to Dick Gamble, who is more than willing."

Rathborne was stung upright. "You wouldn't dare! She's not of age."

"She's of marriageable age if not legal, don't forget that. Now, I've had all I can stomach of you, so get out."

"Your insolence and temerity, Theodore, mitigates to a considerable degree my respect for your age. I have a notion to thrash you within an inch of your life!" Rathborne stood up threateningly, his eyes insane with rage. Suddenly he gasped and drew back in fear as a wicked-looking automatic was aimed with unwavering steadiness at his belt buckle.

"It wouldn't take a really warlike move to motivate this trigger finger, you long-drawn-out pestilence. Just any sort of move would do it. Do you know how long it takes a man to die with a .45 caliber slug in the guts? Days, and in the most excruciating pain. That's where I'm going to plug you, Rathborne—right smack through the neck of the duodenum, and don't think I don't know to the inch where it is. Go on and make your move."

Rathborne's breath fluttered through stricken lips like powdered paper through a suction nozzle, his face the color of a cadaver. I could easily murder him right now, thought the Doctor. Look at his blue lips and strangling breath. Coronary! I could fire and miss him but the shock would kill him and even an autopsy would only reveal heart failure. He raised the gun, pointing it straight at the Minister's eyes.

"Now you can leave, and be quick about it before I yield to a temptation that was just offered to me in a manner that makes it hard to refuse."

The frightened minister tottered from the room, closing the door behind him. He stopped fifty feet from the Doctor's house and leaned giddily against a pecan tree, clinging to it for a long time while the pain in his chest gradually subsided and his starved lungs began to provide oxygen again. He started weakly down the street, still tottery in the legs, but with a course of action fully planned out. He went home and, sitting at his hall table, called a number on the phone.

"I should like to know your opinion of a certain Richard Gamble," he said, carefully altering his voice.

The angry sounds that came through the phone activated his lips into a gratified smile.

"And what would you do for revenge?"

The tones became even more emphatic. He answered a question put to him by the voice.

"Who I am is not important, Miss Hardwicke. I shall contact you later."

Dick, slipping backwards, went again to Abe Mullins' bar because of an order from Dr. Franchette forbidding him any contact with Karel until some mysterious trouble had been cleared up. He was angry and looking for someone upon whom to vent his frustrated spleen. The haunting desire to see the girl mounted within him until he felt the need for partial, if not complete, oblivion and, remembering that Abe would probably only serve him a certain amount of liquor, he bought a pint at the drugstore and put it in his back pocket before he went to the saloon.

He did not see the Reverened Rathborne approach Jack McGrew on the other side of the street, where the latter had been morosely watching the barroom doors, nor would he have given it a second thought, save possibly to wish that Jack would try to start something again. Dick was definitely in the mood for battle.

Abe grinned at him. "Thought you was takin' your business sommers else."

Dick climbed grimly to a stool. "The other places aren't this handy. Gimme a triple shot of bourbon and none of your lip."

"Lip cost you nuthin'," said Abe in no way alarmed. "Likker does."

"I'll pay for the liquor."

"How 'bout some cheeze and crackers? It ain't good to drink lessen you got somethin' in your craw."

"No, thanks. I've had supper. Goddammit, Abe, what have you got against me getting drunk if I want to?"

"Not a thing," said Abe equably. "Thing is though, bub, if Jack ever ketches you drunk and me not around with my mallet, he's likely to chew you up."

Dick felt miserable. "Maybe you better use it on me. Looks like I forget every day what you've done for me."

Abe shrugged. " 'Tain't nuthin'. I allus takes care of my good customers, and my feelin's is tougher'n an elephant's hide."

"They must be. Stand 'er up again … three-timer."

Two hours later Dick was a little tight and Abe lowered the curfew on him. "This'n's on the house, bub, and you know what that means."

Dick nodded affably. "Sure. That's all right, Abe. How about pushing me out a Coke?"

"Sure, if you want it."

Dick cackled gleefully as he took the Coke and pulled the pint from his pocket. "There, wise guy. I outsmarted you this time. The Coke'll last me till this pint's half gone."

"You wouldn't want to make a bet on who outsmarted who, would you … say, two-to-one?"

"Ah-h-h," Dick looked owlishly at his bottle to make sure it hadn't been switched on him. "Thassa bet. Fi' bucks."

"I'll take it. You can pay me in the morning."

"You'll pay *me* in the morning."

"Well, we'll see." The phone rang and Abe picked up the receiver. "Yeah, he's here. Just a minute. Fer you, bub."

"For me? Hell, nobody knows I'm here."

"Somebody seems to."

Dick went behind the bar. "Yeah, it's me. What? Oh, for Christ's sake, why don't you grow up?" He listened for a few minutes. "Oh, okay. I'll see you after I get home. 'Bye."

"Woman, hunh?"

"Yes, dammit. Jack's ladylove. Boy, is she hard to get rid of."

The night was very dark and the only light was the faint radiation of a myriad of stars. Across the street from the Hardwicke house, the Reverend Rathborne stood in the shadow of a big magnolia tree and waited. He had visited the Hardwicke house earlier and had come away in as high a state of elation as he ever allowed himself. He looked at his watch for the tenth time and, his patience fraying, he glanced up and down the street impatiently before darting across and sneaking through Mrs. Pinkney's gate and around the house until he stood outside Dick's room. His height enabled him to peer into a window but he could see nothing.

He gasped as he heard the front door slam and Mrs. Pinkney came on the porch. She belched audibly and began to rock. He glanced at his watch again. Eleven o'clock. What was the woman doing up at this hour? Insomnia, probably. In any event, he would have a hard time explaining his presence if he went out the front way, so he tiptoed across the lawn and vaulted the low, spiked iron fence that separated the Hardwicke property from Mrs. Pinkney's. As he turned, a figure loomed before him, two powerful hands gripped him by the windpipe and the cry that had started was choked off before it could emerge.

Dick, feeling hilariously pickled, shoved the remainder of the pint across the bar, where Abe caught it. "Keep it, y'ole windbag.

We'll sh … slil … dammit, celebrate tomorrow when you p—pay me off."

"Okay. I'll hold it for you. Better watch out fer Jack. He'd clean your plow if he caught you now."

"Who, that big bagger mush? Why I'd …" He swung at an imaginary foe and fell sprawling. "Somebody tripped me."

"Sure did—name of Dick Gamble."

"Goter hell, Abe, y'bassard." He got up and walked unsteadily out of the barroom. As he reached the sidewalk, a car slid up and stopped. "Can I take you some place?" The top was down and Annette looked cool and inviting, her breasts surging against a halter and her lush legs bare where her skimpy shorts failed to cover them.

"Hell, yes. Take me anywhere—jus' so you're there."

They rode east on the smooth concrete. He bent over and kissed the smooth, flawless skin of her thigh. She shuddered and made a little noise that acted as a powerful signal to him. He kissed the thigh again, closer, feeling his hot blood pulsing, stimulated both by the delight of her body and the whiskey he had consumed.

He felt the clutching fingers of near frenzy squeeze him until his ears rang, making him abandon all gentleness, and he forced her to him so strongly that the car began to yaw.

"Please, Dick … please … let me stop the car … Dick!"

It rolled off the low shoulder and into the shallow ditch and on, until some springy youpon bushes stopped it with a whispery crash. Neither of them heard it. Neither of them knew the car had left the road, and neither of them cared.

He tore at her clothes with a fierce urgency that made every second a maddening eternity. She helped him and soon their writhing, wet bodies locked together in a lurching clutch that wrung from her lips an "Oh!" from such inner depths that his already towering passion rose to heights that even he had never dreamed of.

Later, eons later it seemed, he heard his name being called as over a great distance.

"Dick, wake up! Please wake up. It's three o'clock and we have to go home."

He sat up, his head splitting and banging, shaking him with pile-driver blows. "Three?" He leaned back and moaned. "Just let me die. Christ, what a head!"

"I have some aspirin."

"Anything to chase them with?"

"I have a case of beer in the trunk. It was cold when I picked you up. It's for Dad."

It was still cold enough to swallow without gagging him and he washed four aspirin down. "Ride on over to Talapa River and let me catch some air. It isn't far."

Before they reached the river, he felt like a new man and was relatively sober. She slowed down on the bridge where they could see the twin beaches stretching whitely in the starlight.

"What a night for a swim. I need one, too. You know how to get off the road around here?"

"Yes, but shouldn't we go home?" She seemed anxious.

He reached over and stepped on the brake, brought the car to a stop, pulled her to him and gave her a kiss that started his pulses to racing again. "Want to go home now?"

Her eyes were wide and her breath fluttered uncertainly as his hand groped unerringly in the dark. "No ... No, I don't want to go home yet ... Oh ... Dick!"

In the cool water her body was as smooth as a fish and slippery, as though her pores oozed a balmy lubricant. "Dick ... the blanket ... the sand ..." He carried her to the blanket, her skin wet, cool, yet throbbing and eager. Her breasts were like upthrust peaks of ice cream tipped with cherries, taut, heaving, urging themselves against his face, a fervent delight to his eager lips.

CHAPTER ELEVEN

DICK GAMBLE greeted the rising sun with a frown and a groan. His head clanged like a locomotive repair shop and his mouth had an acrid taste. He controlled his stomach with an effort and tottered to the bathroom where he attempted to trade the taste for that of a popular brand of tooth paste, with fair results. He drank a glass of water and promptly threw it up, along with a variety of the previous night's gastronomic intake.

He had just put up his glass and was standing very still, hardly daring to breathe because he had swallowed some aspirins and the slightest move might send them bounding upward again, when a scream tore into his consciousness like the edge of a saw on live flesh. The skin on his neck contacted and a vast armada of goose pimples sprang instantly into being. He leaped from the bathroom with nothing on but a pair of pants and dashed through the house toward the scream. He tripped on the back door threshold and fell, sprawling headlong down the steps, almost knocking Mrs. Pinkney down.

"What's the matter?" he yelled, trying to stop the screams that were coming from the woman's agonized throat with every breath. She grasped a handful of hennaed hair and, whirling in a half circle, fell into his arms—not in a faint because she still continued to scream. He dumped her to the ground abruptly and slapped her a stinging blow in the face that stopped her screams instantly. Then she did faint, but not before making a dramatic gesture toward the fence separating the Hardwicke's yard from her own. Dick froze in his tracks and held the pose for a long moment, his stomach congealing into a solid mass of icy numbness. His tongue seemed to swell and then he realized that he was trying to scream also. So he clamped his jaws shut and, by dint of sheer will, forced himself to walk toward the horrible figure that hung half erect on the sharp spikes of the fence. When he came within ten feet, he recognized the distorted features to be those of the Reverend Rathborne, although he made the identification more by the hair than by the features. Rathborne's thin lips were drawn so far back in a grimace of agony that the gums showed for three-quarters of an inch. His hands were fastened in his shirt or coat—Dick couldn't tell which until he finally saw that they were grasping two bloody spikes that had penetrated his chest, grasping them in the same way that a man mortally wounded by an arrow will grasp the shaft in his death throes. The tall man's knees were buckled and sticking out at wide angles like broken posts, and from the tail of his coat, twin icicles of blood had congealed, trailing all the way to the ground. Dick reeled, caught a spike of the fence as a prop, shuddered violently and let it go with haste. He became very sick and knelt in the dew-damp grass. Janey Hardwicke appeared at that moment on her front porch, pulling a robe around her.

"What is all the racket?" she asked irritably. "Woke me up from a sound sleep. I thought someone was being murdered." She looked queerly at Dick and came down the steps, walking toward him. "What on earth is the matter with you—not that I care, but I'm curious." She stopped with such precipitous suddenness that she almost fell. She took a swift glance at the sight on the fence and went milk white. Her hand groped aimlessly over her breast to her throat and then she, too, screamed and fell with a thud, face down in the grass.

Dick gritted his teeth and forced himself to stand up. He walked back to Mrs. Pinkney, tried to lift her but he was in no condition to raise her flabby weight and so he let her slide back to the ground and went into the house where he called the Sheriff and then Dr. Franchette. Having done what he could, he sat on the old hall sofa and, though the horsehair pricked his back like a cactus burr, he did not feel it, sinking into a sort of stunned semi-coma.

Dr. Franchette applied a match to Fannie Blumendahl's cigarette and sat back, mopping his brow.

"I've been called on to view some pretty awful sights in the course of my medical career, but I'll tell you, what I saw this morning still has me with the jitters."

"Do they have any idea who did it?"

"Not the slightest, unless, of course, that Hardwicke girl isn't telling all she knows. She affects to faint and have hysterics every time someone questions her about it. The Sheriff was inclined to suspect Dick until I pointed out to him that Dick was not likely to kill him, throw him over the fence and then hang him on those spikes like a butcher bird would hang up a tumble bug."

She crossed her legs and sipped at her highball. "What actually killed him?"

"Several things could have. He had been choked with such force that his thyroid was a pulp, several tracheal cartilages crushed, and, of course, there were the spikes of the fence, two of them, either of which would have killed him instantly. One cut the aorta not two inches from his heart and the other went through the upper right quadrant of the lung. It was evident that whoever did it was a man of extraordinary strength. He had simply been shoved on those spikes by brute force." The Doctor bobbled his beard rapidly and began to pat his pockets for a cheroot, which he finally found and lit. "I'll tell you," he continued, "It gave me a turn when I went over there. He was still hanging on those spikes, like a dummy someone had carelessly tossed away and had accidentally hung on the fence." He looked up and Fannie's face was split wide with an enormous grin. "Well," he snapped irritably, "what is so dad-blasted funny?"

She burst out laughing. "I'm laughing at me."

"A laugh of that sort I could join with gusto," he said offensively, "if I knew the joke."

"Oh…nothing much. I was just sitting here thinking just how our sisters of Faith, Hope and Charity would react if they knew what unalloyed joy that old rail's demise gives me. I ain't a damn bit sorry. I'm tickled half pink and, to you at least, I'm admitting it freely. Think of it. Some good angel just grabbed the old hypocrite and spitted him on that iron fence like a roasting pig."

"Sometimes," he said, eyeing her critically, "I am forced to think that you are as calloused as the skin on a circus monkey's behind."

As soon as Dick got free of the Sheriff's questioning, he went to work and was excused for the day by Jeff Peters. "Nuthin' pressin', son. Go on and try to get your nerves in shape."

"That's all right," said Dick, sitting at his desk. "I'll be all right." He picked up a vase with a dead flower in it, thinking he would throw the flower in the wastebasket, and it slipped from his shaking fingers, shattering to bits on the concrete floor. He sat still, gazing stupidly at the fragments, as Jeff laughed.

"Sure. You're as steady as the courthouse. Better take my advice and take the day off. 'Tain't every day a man wakes up with a murdered preacher in his back yard."

Sensing the wisdom of Jeff's words, Dick put away the papers he had taken from the files and walked out, heading for Abe Mullins' place instinctively. He walked in wearily and sat at the bar without even troubling to look about, not wanting a drink but feeling the need to talk to a man with Abe's understanding.

"What the hell's all that ruckus up the hill this morning?" asked Abe with a glance at a man who sat at the other end of the bar, gazing moodily into a glass of whiskey. "I ain't had but one customer this mornin' and…" He leaned over, lowering his voice. "… If you don't want no trouble, you'd better beat it before he…"

Dick glanced at the other man who, at the same time, glanced at him. Jack McGrew leaped to his feet with a hoarse scream, his face livid with fear, and started backing away. "No! No… You're…" He wheeled around and ran headlong into the brick wall of the rear of the saloon, his head cracking soddenly against the masonry. He bounded back, sobbing, saliva drooling on long ropes from his lips, and rammed the wall again. This time he slid to the floor and lay there quietly.

Dick felt the hair rise on his head. "Holy Cats, what's the matter with him?"

Abe mopped sweat from his broad face. "Goddamighty… I don't know. He's gone nuts for sure this time. D'ja ever see a man take a rap like that on his head and then turn right around and do it again? I better call the Sheriff."

"Before you do, slide me a triple out here. I've had about all I can take for one day without some help." Dick gulped the drink down and swallowed water to keep it in place, his eyes straying back to the figure on the floor which had regained a semblance of consciousness. McGrew crawled painfully up the wall and began to caress it with both hands, mouthing incoherencies, whining and begging the wall not to hurt him again. He staggered to his feet, passed a shaking hand over his eyes that had now taken on the dead stare of an unconscious person. He turned away from the wall and, lurching over to the bar, stood there staring at Dick, breathing hard, his mouth still open and drooling.

Dick felt a shuddering wave of revulsion wash over him. "Sheriff coming?" he asked over his shoulder.

Abe put the phone down. "Yeah. Be here in a minute."

Jack began to talk in a whining, placating monotone. "Didn't mean it, Gamble… didn't mean it at all. Shouldn't have killed you, Gamble, shouldn't have killed you. Sorry I killed you, but I had to, Gamble. I had to… dark and couldn't see very well…"

His voice trailed off and he leaned heavily against the bar. "Didn't want to kill anybody ... didn't want to kill anybody ... didn't want to kill anybody ..." His voice grew weaker, finally dying into a whisper, and again he fell full length on the floor.

"Rathborne! He killed Rathborne!" Dick was pointing a shaking finger at the man on the floor.

"Was that what all the ruckus was about? Well, I ... I mean, that was what I was askin' you a while ago. What happened?"

Dick shuddered and shoved the glass across the bar eloquently. When it was filled, he took a sip and said. "Rathborne ... stuck on those steel pickets at Hardwicke's ... stuck there like a side of beef. All blood, his face ... God!" He took out his handkerchief and wiped the clammy sweat from his face.

The Sheriff walked in and took off his hat, mopping his brow with a blue bandanna. "Christ, what a day. First Rathborne then—That's Jack there, ain't it?" They nodded.

"He's gone slap off his onion," said Abe. "Tried to butt the back end out of my place. Wonder he didn't fracture his skull. Better take him to the Clinic. By the way, he's your murderer."

The Sheriff straightened up. *"What?"*

Abe nodded. "It was last night and he thought it was bub here. When he saw Dick come in, he yelled like a panther and rammed that wall back there where you see the bloody spot. That's where he rammed it the second time. Seein' Dick mighty nigh skeered him to death. He got up after a while and come to where you see him now. Said he was sorry he had killed 'im. That's the way I got it figured out. Moon didn't rise last night till around two o'clock. It was as dark as the inside of a stovepipe up till then. Rathborne musta went there for some reason and Jack thought he was Dick."

Williams put his hat on and motioned toward the phone. "Call Happy and tell him to bring the ambulance over. Hope Dr. Albert can bring him to so's I can question him. I'm beginnin't' smell sumpn' here, what with this, that and the other."

"Don't know how much weight it'll have. Man's crazy as a well fulla bats."

The Sheriff took off his hat and scratched his head. "Mebby so, but if he can give me a lead, it'll help. Maybe I can pull sumpn' that'll git the evidence for me."

The ambulance pulled up and two minutes later whined away, bearing the limp body of Jack McGrew.

Dick drained his whiskey glass and pushed it across the bar. "Do it again."

Abe shook his head. "The way you're goin! Say, what'd you have for breakfast?"

"Didn't eat any ... couldn't."

"What I thought. Wait a minnit. I'll fix you somethin'."

He returned five minutes later with a rugged sandwich made of ham, cheese, dill pickles and homemade bread. "My old lady baked that there bread this mornin'—best you ever et." He poured out a tall glass of cold milk. "Now get that inside you and forget about any more drinkin'."

Dick complied meekly and after eating the sandwich and milk, he felt a lot better. "I think I'll make it all right now, Abe."

"Sure you will. Ever'thing's all over now."

Dick, once the phrenetic excitement of the murder had died down, went to see Dr. Franchette, his jaw set and his mind made up. He had hardly accepted the chair Theodore set out for him when he said, "I'm going to see Karel tonight."

"I don't think you are," said the Doctor softly, so softly that Dick was taken aback.

"But ... I've been hearing things, Dr. Franchette. I had an idea that the 'trouble' you mentioned yesterday had to do with Karel's grandfather."

"You are quite correct."

Dick's anger began to rise. "Then the trouble is done with. The man is dead, or are you pretending great sorrow?"

"No, I'm not pretending any sorrow. I think his death has simplified matters considerably."

"Then I'm going to see her."

"And I say that you are not."

Dick's jaw grew hard and his chin inched forward. "I suppose you have a reason for making so flat a statement?"

"I do. I despise to have to treat you like an adolescent but since you insist on acting like one, I have no choice. I think the seediest character ever whelped would have enough good taste not to force himself on a girl immediately after her grandfather was brutally murdered. This has nothing to do with her feelings toward him. The fact remains that Rathborne was Karel's grandfather, and he was murdered. I doubt that anyone is 'pretending' any sorrow about the man's death, but I can recall that you were in a state of what we shall charitably call nerves when I arrived at your house this morning—Even you, who had no real connection with this thing. It shouldn't fall to me to have to give you a lesson in good taste, something you should have absorbed from your fellows, something your parents should have taught you—but since Karel is involved, I'll take on the job. I might point out to you while I'm at it that you hardly measure up to what Fannie and I would like to see the girl acquire as a lifetime mate. Nevertheless, we are willing to give you a chance. It would be no more than fair to tell you, however, that if you do not begin very soon to show some of the symptoms of manhood, you might as well forget the girl. You have seen us operate and I think you can appreciate what I mean."

Crushed, humiliated and sick with a sickness of such acrid bitterness that he could hardly see, Dick made his way to the street and stood there, striving by deep-breathing exercises to regain some semblance of his aplomb. He had progressed to the point that he did not argue with the Doctor either directly or within himself. The old man had spoken no less than the truth. The desire to see the girl, now that all obstacles had been removed, had driven every other consideration from his mind. It had not occurred to him that Rathborne's death was of sufficient importance that he should not see Karel immediately. Then he remembered that this was Louisiana, where respect for the dead is often revealed in bizarre gestures even though no feeling is present; Louisiana, where anything that happens within the family circle must bend to protocol, regardless of personal private feelings.

"I'm in love," he countered fiercely. "Everything falls before love, no matter what it is." He swallowed and threw back his shoulders. He'd see how far they'd get in trying to stop him. He'd prove that love was victor above all, here as elsewhere. He'd see what Theodore Franchette would do, what Fannie Blumendahl would do.

Had he been less in willful love and more acute in sharp perception, he might have found it peculiar that, to all intents and purposes, they had done nothing. Fannie even rose to greet him at the steps.

"Come on in, son. Karel is in the parlor. I assume that's who you came to see."

"Yes," he said almost rudely. "That's who I came to see."

"Go on in. She'll be glad to see you, I suppose."

He glanced at her sharply and then walked on through the huge twin doors. What had she meant, saying she supposed Karel would be glad to see him?

"Good evening, Karel."

She closed the record album and put it away before going over to him. "I'm glad to see you, Dick."

"I knew you would be," he said exultantly. "That old Doctor doesn't know everything."

"What did he say?"

"He said it wasn't good taste to visit you so soon after your grandfather ... er ... died."

She was silent for a moment, opening her lips to speak but closing them again. "Sit down, Dick."

He sat on the couch she offered and made room for her. "I'm glad all this is over, Karel, and we can make our plans. Now, I don't intend to be a bookkeeper all my life. In fact, I…" He stopped and caught his breath. He hadn't the faintest idea of what he could be because he had never been anything. "Anyway," he continued, dismissing the problem with an airy wave of his hand, "I'll get into something and make a lot of money and—why. What's the matter?"

Her teeth gleamed pearl-white in the soft light from the hand-painted parchments that covered the lamps.

"You sound like a little boy promising to be an engineer and bring home everything to Mommy."

Dick's face flamed hot and tight, making him earnestly desire to hide in a deep, dark closet. "I sounded bad, did I?"

"No, not bad … just very young and immature." She frowned and her lips compressed, forming a straight line. "I think I know what's the matter with you, Dick. You *are* young—and I don't mean in years."

His jaw grew hard. "What do you mean?"

"I mean that you came in here after Dr. Franchette told you not to. That wasn't too bad because actually I'm not sad. I'm just shocked and unstrung. You should have known that without anyone having to tell you. Then you come in here and start making plans. Plans for what?"

"Well, holy mackerel, Karel," he burst out furiously, "don't you know?"

"No, I don't know."

He held his breath and glared at her. "In words of two syllables, I want you to marry me."

She nodded slowly. "You … I think you do. You, you, you. That's all you think about. You are the great 'I'—the one and only. You come in here and immediately make plans to marry me."

She stood up and Dick got his second glance of the arctic gates closing in his face. The chill from her green eyes made a ripple thread its way through his nerves.

"Are you a complete fool? Dash in here and we'll plan everything. You want me to marry *you*. It isn't 'let's get married' or 'will you be my wife', it's 'marry me.' Do you realize that you never even asked me if I'd marry you? Do you realize that you have never told me that you love me? Tell me, what on earth even gave you the idea that I was in such dire straits that I'd walk into something like this? Yes-Dick-this, yes-Dick-that, never asking a question, picking up whatever crumbs you tossed out and being overwhelmed by marrying the great Dick Gamble." She stopped and considered him gravely. "I think the best thing for you to do is to go back and talk to Dr. Franchette again. I'm not nineteen yet, but I had more sense at the age of twelve than you do right now. Thanks for giving me the first chance—or is it the first? In any event, I don't care for any and now I think you'd better go. Social visits are frowned on at such times as this. My grandfather was killed last night."

Dick finally got his car under way. He had no feelings, no thoughts, no volition. He was a zombie, a sleepwalker automatically driving a car. He ran into a small steer on the other side of the creek bridge and bent a fender down on a wheel. He had to get out to pull it up before he could continue, and he cut his hand badly. His senses were so dulled with shock, however, that he hardly felt the pain, although the profuse bleeding made him wrap his handkerchief around it to keep from messing up his clothes. He pulled the car up in a vacant spot in front of Abe Mullins' place and walked slowly in.

"Hey, bub, you cut yourself."

Dick stared vacantly at the blood-soaked handkerchief. "Yeah, sure did ... triple."

"Comin' up. What you got the pips about?"

"Er, what?"

"What you got the red butt about?"

Dick stared at him for a moment. "What did you say, Abe?"

Abe stared back. "What'n hell's the matter with you? Sick?"

"No, I feel fine."

"You look like you was shot at and missed. Sure you're all right?"

"What?" His stare was foggy and opaque.

"Nuthin,' 'cept you better go see Dr. Albert with that hand. You must be about to bleed to death."

"You'd bleed to death, too, with two of those fence spikes rammed through you."

Abe glanced at his mallet, gripped his temper figuratively in both hands and put his face within inches of Dick's. "Is you got two rods rammed through you?"

"Of course not. What made you think so? This little scratch on my hand?"

Abe turned around, poured out four fingers of bourbon and threw them down in a gulp. He drummed on the counter and glowered at Dick, who had gone back into his trance and was looking into his glass with a fixed stare. Several other customers, collected at the other end of the bar and throwing dice for beer, ignored them. Abe sighed, shook his head and poured Dick another drink without ever taking the glass from between his hands. If Dick saw the act, he paid no attention but drank it dutifully. An hour later he was sodden from a number of drinks but still dazed and motionless on his stool.

Dr. Franchette, after having been called to the hospital to assist his son in sewing up a serious knife wound, was now on his way home, tired and cursing under his breath. "Evening, Abe. I'll take—"

"Bradsher's Special Age and ginger ale with a twist of lime peel. You don't hafta tell me, Doc. How big this time?"

"Put it in the biggest glass you have and build it to scale ... Oh, hello, Dick. You were so quiet that I didn't see you."

Dick looked up stupidly at the mention of his name and stared as though the other were a total stranger. Then he began to show some animation. "You did it," he said thickly.

"Very likely," said Franchette agreeably. "Did what?"

"Karel. She…I went there…tonight. She told me to go away." His movements were slow and mechanical as he stood up and advanced toward the Doctor. "You did it. You—" He drew back his right with precise deliberation but it never started forward. A ham-like hand fastened itself in his shirt front and he went up in the air with the greatest of ease, was twirled about just in time to meet the other hand doubled into a fist approximately the consistency of a baked oak knot. There was a brilliant spurt of varicolored lights and then deep, soft peace and a sensation of falling a great distance.

"That eight-inch insulation of suet you've gathered in the last ten years doesn't seem to have slowed you down, Abe," said the Doctor with a chuckle. "If memory serves me right, you rescued me once before in this very spot. Oil rig gentleman, I believe it was. I then had to sew up a two-inch gash in his chin."

Abe massaged the knuckles of his hand and turned to his curious customers. "Just drink right on," he said easily. "A little exercise, that's all." There were several ironic laughs but the men went back to their drinking.

Dick began to stir after a few minutes and finally he sat up and felt gingerly of his jaw. "You hit me," he said accusingly to Abe.

"I sure did, bub. You drawed back at a man old enough to be your grandpa. He brung all three of my kids and he ain't ever sent me a bill yet. You're lucky I didn't break your goddam neck. Now that you done come to, you can beat it. I can do without your business from now on. In fact, I'm tellin' you right now— don't never poke your half-growed nose in my place again. Next time I'll spread you all over the floor."

Dick climbed to his feet and looked at Dr. Franchette, who leaned against the bar sipping his drink. "You—"

"No, *you!* Let's not confuse the issue... you, in capitals. When you told me those things the other day, I was beginning to think that you had made the grade. I find I was wrong. When you feel that you can call yourself a man, let me know and we'll see."

Dick's left hand fluttered aimlessly and finally went into his pocket. He turned and went out of the door, his steps dragging and his shoulders slumped.

"Reckon we was too hard on him—busted his spirit or somethin'?"

"He has no lack of spirit. What he needs is courage—Cuts, in other words—but it'll take a lot of boiling to stew the fact into his head that there are other people in the world. He vaguely knows there are but he can't seem to realize that he isn't the only one that matters."

CHAPTER TWELVE

WINTER came late, as it does in Louisiana, after the usual parade of chilly mornings and warm, dry days that chilled again toward sunset. As Dr. Franchette walked up the path to Fannie Blumendahl's house, however, the weather was the sort he detested. A dull, gray pall hung over the world and a damp, irritating wind blew steadily out of the north. He hugged his topcoat to his hips and quickened his stride. As he walked up on the verandah, Fannie opened the door. "Well bust my buttons, look who braved the icy blasts to—"

"A pox on such weather," he complained testily. "A pox on you for a noisy, blathering female ... Fmmmf, do I smell hot, buttered rum?"

"You do unless your smeller has gone bad on you, and it looks like it hasn't. *Lula!*"

Her voice shattered the quiet of the house like a field gun at sunset. Lula poked her head into the parlor. "Ma'am?"

"Bring Dr. Franchette a hot rum. Rum it good for him."

When the drink came, he carefully arranged the napkin around the brown stone mug and inhaled gratefully. "Ah ... What is it the vintners buy half so precious as the stuff they sell?"

"Search my soul. I never ran a store where they hang out."

He looked briefly at heaven, shrugged, tasted his rum and smacked his lips delicately.

"I should have known not to wax romantic to the point of the Rubaiyat to you. Your soul is cold and—"

"That's not what's cold about you, you tottering old wreck."

"Leave us not indulge in personalities," he protested mildly. "Where is Karel?"

"She's around. She's been reading too much."

"What makes you say that?"

"Oh, youngsters stay too quiet when they read and I get the fidgits. More of that 'Aching Arms' poetry has been turning up lately. I don't like it."

"Neither do I. What I'd like is for her to get interested in some deserving boy."

"I think she still thinks about Gamble. Tell me, what's exactly wrong with that lad? He seemed to have a lot of the necessary ingredients."

"He did indeed. However, as a cook you must know what happens when you have only ingredients. It takes some careful mixing to make a good cake. His quantities were all wrong, too much of this, not enough of that. He just wasn't ready for baking."

"What happened to him?"

"He left. Went back to his aunt's and stayed there about a week—stayed drunk the whole time, then left. He is now working with a drilling crew in Terrebonne Parish."

"How the devil do you know all that?"

Dr. Franchette decorated his face with a smile of superiority. "You have stooges in this parish. I have stooges all over the South. I keep my fingers on the pulse of the—"

Fannie uttered a very unladylike word and then added, "Nuts. Someone told you."

"But certainly. I didn't say they didn't. The best spies in the world are people."

"You're an ass. Do you think the boy will come back?"

"On a guess, I'd say yes. Actually, I don't know that I want him back here till he gets a grip of sorts on himself. His youth was...I don't know what it was except that nothing seemed to stick to him. Since then he has learned slowly and painfully but every time things get rough, his bullheaded pride always gets the upper hand and he shorts out."

"Fool pride, as my pop used to say. Look, I'm throwing a sort of private fandang here at Christmas and we'd like to have all of you out. You, Maude, Albert and Lisabeth."

"Ummm, Christmas ... that's ten days off. I think Albert can make it. He let Jenkins have Thanksgiving off so he could have Christmas. We had planned—"

"Unplan it. I know damn well Maude doesn't want to slave over that antique stove she has and you're too tight to hire a cook. All of you come on Christmas Eve and we'll just have a regular hell buster. Tell Albert, if he can't come that night, to come the next morning. I have presents for all of you and we can stay up late and sleep in late."

Theodore grinned and stroked his beard. "You talked us into it. Sounds good to me."

"All right, we'll expect you."

Christmas Eve was about as cold as it ever gets in South Louisiana. Rain, driven almost horizontal by a half gale, stung like shot and froze almost the instant it touched an object. Mixed in with it were errant particles of sleet that whispered through the grass and against the sides of buildings. At five o'clock that afternoon Dr. Franchette, Maude and Lisabeth slithered to a stop in front of Fahenstock and waited while Bessie and Lula ran out with a tremendous wagon umbrella.

"Huddle up under that tarp, kids," Fannie bellowed from the verandah where she stood in a leather coat, jodhpurs and a man's hunting cap, "or you'll all catch pneumonia. Look out, Maude, that damn walk is as slick as two eels."

"Please spare us your ribald metaphors," shrilled Theodore, struggling to keep from being lifted and blown away by the wind tugging at the giant umbrella.

"Look out, panty waist," yelled Fannie, doubling up with mirth. "That parachute'll take you all the way to Baton

Rouge. Come on in, all of you, and get something warm inside you."

"The devil take it," panted the Doctor, handing the umbrella to the two maids. "I don't want anything warm. I want something warming. Something warm always reminds me of bullion, gruel or soft-boiled eggs, all of which I detest."

"That's just about all you can eat now," jibed Fannie as she led the way into the parlor that was ablaze with candles, Christmas tree and an oak log fire that glowed like a blast furnace.

"Better not sit too close to that fire," warned Fannie. "When that green oak gets going, it'll make you sit back."

"Where's Karel?" asked Maude, looking around.

"Yes, where is she?" seconded Dr. Franchette eagerly.

Fannie looked at him queerly. "She's upstairs. She'll be down shortly."

Supper was succulent barbecued chicken, hot biscuits, chilled raw vegetables with cheese sauce and mayonnaise. After dinner there was *café Brulot* and/or *crème de menthe,* with promise of more to come later. Karel was dressed in a long-sleeved green jersey dress that clung to her figure with such breath-taking enthusiasm that even the women found it difficult to keep their eyes from her. Dr. Franchette, not concerned with such obstacles as sex, didn't even try. She ate quietly, joining in the laughter, but rarely offering anything of her own. Her eyes sparkled, somnolent green, like a pair of fabulous emeralds in the candle light, that also drew radiant gleams from her shimmering hair. Dr. Franchette looked at her keenly and then turned his eyes back to his drink while he digested what he had seen. He sighed and bobbled his beard.

"I thought I detected a curious note in your voice," said Fannie in an undertone, bending toward him, "when you asked where Karel was."

"You … er … did? Well, well, imagine that. Ha-ha!"

"Ha-ha, my foot. What was the meaning of it?"

"I felt a bout of heartburn coming on. It changed my voice."

"I didn't notice it changing your appetite and, personally, I don't think you ever had heartburn in your life."

Dr. Franchette swirled the ice around and sucked up the last drop of *crème de menthe*. "All things come to he who waits," he said cryptically, eyeing the ceiling and making exasperating motions with his chin whiskers.

"I ain't a he!" she exploded. She cringed and looked about guiltily while all the others stopped talking and looked at her. "Sorry, but this old bastard gets me all riled up sometimes." Then, her voice toned down to a modest rumble, "I ought to twist a flipper offa you."

He giggled. "I didn't do a thing."

"You still haven't answered my question."

"I'll quote you another apothegm having to do with the virtue of patience—"

"I ain't got enough patience…" she turned and smiled an apology at the others "…to put in a hollow tooth. I want to know what the hell you got on your mind."

"I promise to tell you before the night is over."

Fannie relaxed and sipped coffee in which burned Napoleon brandy. "Very well. I guess I'd better shut up. Maude and Lisabeth think I'm nuts, yelling at you like that."

"It shows a marked lack of respect besides a certain magpie tendency which you exhibit at times."

"Oh, shut up. Want some coffee?"

"Yes. Virginal coffee. Some that hasn't taken up evil ways with whiskey or brandy. Virgin—"

"First time I ever knew anything virginal to attract you except to render it unvirgin."

"You malign me. You—"

"Oh, be quiet. You're driveling again. Lula, bring Dr. Franchette some coffee…virginal."

Lula brought the coffee and as she placed it in front of him she managed to nudge his shoulder, making him look up. He caught the infinitesimal nod, quickly averted his eyes and ladled sugar into his coffee. After supper they went into the parlor and sat in a semi-circle about the big fire where an argument ensued as to whether the presents should be opened now or the next morning. "I think we should open 'em now," blared Fannie. "If there's anyone able to get up and open presents in the morning, I'll feel that I've failed as a hostess. Let's get 'em open now while we can have a little enthusiasm."

The empress had spoken so they all clustered about the Christmas tree, chattering and trying to guess the contents of various gaily wrapped packages that were strewn in profusion beneath the tree. Fannie went to her knees and began to paw through them, announcing names and handing out presents to the proper owners.

"Lula?"

"Yass'm."

"This is yours. Don't let Lazarus tear them up the first time he pulls 'em off you."

Bessie let go a peal of laughter that would have done justice to Fannie herself and Lula strove to blush through her pigment, turning a rich rosy bronze.

"Bessie, what the hell are you laughing at? Here's one for you. It's a robe and won't need tearing off. It'll save Sammy no end of trouble."

Lula let go a vengeful laugh and together Bessie and Lula opened their packages with exclamations of delight.

"Here's two more for you," said Fannie, handing them each another package. "Now ..." She picked up a package, studied the card on it and then looked at Dr. Franchette, whose face was as bland and innocent as a cup of warm milk. Fannie, not to be outdone, raised her voice in a lusty shout.

"Phillip Richard Gamble."

"Here." Dick moved in from the hall, dressed in a neat, dark blue suit that fitted him in figures well over the hundred-dollar mark. His shoes were handsome, his shirt snowy, and his tie of diagonal blue and white stripes was impeccable. There was a moment's silence during which he stood several feet away from the group, a half-smile on his face. He was tense, watchful and not entirely at ease.

"Well, dammit, take your present and sit down. There are a lot more."

Lisabeth, who was about to rush forward to ease his embarrassment, didn't have a chance because Karel was there ahead of her. "I'm glad to see you, Dick." She took his hand and squeezed it.

"I'm glad to see you," he said, his voice husky and obviously under tight control.

"Here's the rest of your presents," said Fannie, taking them an armload. "You two can get the hell out of the way now and let the rest of us have some room."

Back at the fire, sitting as close together as their chairs would permit, Karel asked, "What happened, Dick?"

"Well, I left Kenton never intending to return. That wasn't the first stupid idea I had, by any means. I went into the oil fields and worked my fool head off trying to forget you."

"And did you?"

"No, I couldn't. It got so bad that I couldn't even get a decent night's sleep. Finally, I knew I'd have to come back. I knew I couldn't stand it any longer and I think that was what really taught me."

"Taught you what?" she asked gently.

He shrugged. "I only know that knowledge and understanding are relative. Compared to the old me, I'm a lot wiser and, I suppose, a lot older. I'll make more mistakes and I'll have more trouble settling my sense of values because, as Dr. Franchette pointed out yesterday, long ago I conditioned all my reflexes into their old way of thinking and acting. I'll have to re-educate them." He fidgeted nervously and then faced her squarely. "Karel, I don't know when we can get alone. I want to marry you as soon as you—" He broke off and smiled. "If, of course, you love me. I remember, that was one of the things that made you sore."

She smiled in return. "Yes, but you should see the you I see now as compared to the you I saw before."

"Then you aren't angry any more?"

"No. I wasn't then, the way you think. You had disappointed me and I was angry at myself, angry at fate and, of course, I was angry at you, too, but the other reasons figured as well."

He caught his breath, still not having his answer and not knowing how to broach the subject again without seeming insistent. She saw the reaction and placed a warm hand on his, her eyes lifting to meet his own with gentle steadiness, "Yes, Dick."

The others were too close. Dick seemed to collapse in his chair from the sudden and complete relief from all tension and pain. They were too close to...He closed his eyes, his breath coming in deep, forced respiration, and from beneath the lids two hot tears crept forth and slid down his cheeks. He fought them away with his handkerchief, angry and embarrassed, but he had been unable to stop them.

"That's all right, darling," she said softly. "Tears are nothing to be ashamed of ... Oh, let's get out of here."

"Where?"

"Lula built a fire in the den. I wondered why at the time. Dr. Franchette must have told her to."

"Well," said Fannie, getting to her feet, "let's go back to the fire and open some of these things. Oh, what do you know? They're gone."

"Hardly a surprising phenomenon," observed Maude as she shook one of her packages gently.

"Damn if you didn't sound just like your husband then."

"And what," he said, "is bad about that?"

"This is Christmas," said Fannie. "Peace on earth and all that guff. Wasn't for that, I'd tell you in great detail."

Dick followed the girl into the cheery room lit by ruddy flames. He felt sick, a trembling deep-seated sickness that fogged his mind and cut off any plans for taking Karel into his arms. If he didn't do this, he felt that he would soon lose control and break down, weeping or wringing his hands to try to ease the exquisite torture of being with her and yet not being able to touch her. She closed the door and faced him, her eyes wide with hungry entreaty, her lips parted and richly red in the firelight. For a moment they looked at each other and then, with a throaty little sound, she went into his arms. All the pent-up misery, the starvation of months, years, flowed between them in thundering cataracts, shaking them soul deep, the release sending out emanations of frenzied emotion. From sheer fatigue and breathlessness they finally drew apart and looked at each other in that wondering disbelief that springs from the fear that something is wrong, that such dreams cannot be true, that they will suddenly crash and chill darkness will again spring up to envelope everything.

Dick stroked the curve of her cheeks with tender, unbelieving hands, his breast aching and tears not far away. He realized how loneliness could take bizarre ways of manifesting itself. How had he ever thought himself self-sufficient?

His fingers still retained a taste of the symmetry and exquisite musculature of her back, the sinuous smoothness of her body beneath her dress, the close fit of the strap of her brassiere and the aching sweetness of her skin.

They sat on the couch in front of the fire. Karel kicked off her shoes, climbed across his lap and lay in the crook of his left arm, relaxing like a child. Her hair fell across his arm in rapids of glistening silk, exposing the soft, pure column of her neck. Her legs glistened dully, encased in lacquered sheaths of nylon, an ivory-tan collar of velvety skin showing where her skirt had slipped up past her stockings.

Like the limb of a robot, his hand moved slowly until it covered the peeping collar of skin, his arm leaping to the shock of the contact. He felt her tense in his arms and then urge herself closer as her arms grew tighter about him. He raised her and their lips met, parted and traded entrances, eliciting little guttural sounds of ecstatic hunger. His hand covered one of her firm, ripe breasts, making her take her mouth from his to freeing it for the gulps of air that her lungs demanded. Suddenly she tightened her grip on him for a moment, and then sat up. With hands that sped about like mice, she opened the front of her dress and unsnapped the catch of her brassiere.

The touch of her breasts was almost more than he could stand, driving him a little mad. He doubled his efforts, drinking in the ceaseless reaction of her body that his caresses stimulated.

He caressed her with his lips, teasing her skin into raptures that made shudders flit over her and her teeth clench to choke back moans that she could not help.

His hand explored twin, ineffably smooth pathways into a darkness that dwindled until at last it was no more and the pathways were no longer twins, merging into a junction that was fitted skin-tight with a sheer white web that was merely a gesture, enticing more than obscuring. The hand halted while Dick held her closer, savoring the whimpering frenzy that kept her in a state of continual subtle movement. A muffled cry burst from her lips ... she pressed her face hard against his breast to stifle it. "Dick ... Oh, Dick!" Her voice urged him toward further exploration while his head swam giddily with what he must do or go mad. "Karel, I'm afraid—"

With a lithe flounce she stood up, rearranged her clothes and then collapsed into a shuddering heap on her knees by the couch. For a moment she fought valiantly for control, then, standing up again, she breathed deeply and patted her hair into place. "I'll have to repair my lipstick. I'll be back in a moment."

"As I have always said, Theodore," Fannie was saying, "there never was a deal that you ever worked on that I couldn't have put down in half the time. Any man dealing with human problems is just three times better off with a woman behind him, or, as in the case of me, in front of him … Hello, Karel. Why, child, you look radiant."

They turned to look at her as Fannie stood and went toward her. "May I speak to you a moment, Fannie, please?"

"Of course." They went into the hall, Fannie closing the door behind her. "I know—you're in love, Karel."

She sobbed briefly on Fannie's large chest and then nodded. "So much in love that I think it'll kill me."

"Rarely happens, child. Now, what's on your mind?"

"Will Dick spend the night here?"

In one brilliant flash, Fannie, who was not very slow regarding such things, understood, sympathized and approved. "Yes, of course. He'll take the green room. Right next to yours, Karel."

The girl's eyes shot upward and looked into those of the older woman. She drew a ragged breath, seeing complete understanding, complete knowledge and no sign of disapproval.

She moved a hand over her forehead, her eyes seeking Fannie's again. "Fannie … you know?"

Fannie's voice was a caress, a whispered note from a cello. "Of course I know. I'm an old woman, Karel. I know most things where young people are concerned because I haven't forgotten my own youth."

"You haven't even lost it," Karel said. "You still have it."

"Just the memory," Fannie smiled gently. "It happens that the people in this house tonight are of a precious few, unspoiled by their association with fools and idiots. You may retire when you are ready, my dear. They'll excuse you. You may show Dick to his room."

The girl shook her head slowly. "I can hardly believe that you could look at me and know—and then, after knowing, be actually approving."

"Look," Fannie's voice grew rough and hard. "You've been unhappy. You've loved the boy for a long time. This is the moment of your triumph…take it for everything that is in it. The legal mumbo-jumbo that'll follow is a part of it but totally unrelated to what will happen to you. To wait for it is like waiting to wash your feet before eating and letting the fish spoil. You go ahead…follow your nose and no one will interfere. Goodnight, Daughter."

"Goodnight, Mother…the most wonderful mother any girl ever had."

"Oh, go along with you…" Fannie sniffed, turned about and slammed the door behind her with a crash that made Lula strangle on a drink of pilfered whiskey a hundred feet away in the kitchen.

She stood for a moment looking into the questioning eyes of her guests, unmindful of the tears that coursed down her plump cheeks. "Merry Christmas," she roared. "Goddammit, Theodore, quit looking so insufferably smug and superior. You didn't have a thing to do with it and you don't even know—" She stopped because she had a peculiar feeling that he did know.

Back in the den Karel stood between Dick and the fire. "Dick, you're to stay the night…in the green room…next to mine."

He stood up, his eyes wide with amazement. "You saw Fannie, didn't you?"

"Yes."

"She told you that?"

"Yes."

He passed a hand over his eyes and sank back on the couch. "I guess I don't know much about people even yet."

"Dick…come up here." He stood up and she went into his arms, holding him close, letting him drink in the warm soft wonder of her quiescent body, fitting it to him with eagerness not unmixed with a sweet surrender. "I'll show you your room now."

"Our room, darling."

She nodded. "Our room."

Back in the living room Fannie was getting slightly glassy-eyed.

"What ever happened to Jack McGrew, Theodore?"

He tapped a length of ash from his cheroot and bobbed his beard. "In Jackson, where he should have been ten years ago. He was dangerous, psychotic and yet, because he was a McGrew, no one ever suggested putting him there. Did you know that he serviced Janey Hardwicke at the age of eleven? He called it rape when the Sheriff questioned him and I dare say Janey called it that, too, although I have some doubts. She used him as a sort of handy stallion from time to time and had him eating out of her hand. She put him up to tackling Dick, only Rathborne turned up in the dark and got what was intended for Dick. The fact that he was there raises a number of questions that'll never be answered. Janey isn't talking, and what with Jack's mental condition, no one will ever know whether or not Rathborne had a hand in the matter. I rather believe he had because I had told him that I'd marry Karel to Dick before I'd let him have her."

"You," pointed out Lisabeth, "might be a murderer."

"If he is," retorted Fannie, "he's worth more in that role than he ever was before."

"Oh, he used to have his points," objected Maude mildly.

"I'm glad you said that. I was doubting that the old relic was ever anything but an old relic."

"Go ahead, you two, and rend me. My gentlemanly instincts dictate that I do not rend back."

Dick had showered and was walking up and down in the room, clad in the crimson robe Dr. Franchette had given him for Christmas. He was in a fever of anticipation, his mind revolving madly and his nerves shrieking for release. He held them down with an iron hand but he felt that if she didn't hurry, he'd lose his grip. The room was softly luminous and a gas log hissed in the fireplace, sending off warmth that contrasted snugly with the sleety tinkle on the windows, the moaning of the wind.

She came through the door soundlessly, draped in a white wraith of a creation that was there and yet not there. She stood still for a moment, seeming to be a smoky dream of unreality, a delicate color photograph viewed through milky glass. The tips of her breasts were rose pink, large and erect from the ceaseless throb of passion that was shaking her and the chilling realization that at last nothing would stop them. Dick stood transfixed, devouring every line of her body, revealed and yet not revealed by the thin fabric that enveloped her like a lamp shade covers the bulb, misting it and yet allowing illumination to shine through. With a sob he sprang forward and caught her in his arms and was enveloped by that warm human smell—the exotic perfume that man has never been able to reproduce—the heady fragrance of a clean, passionate woman. His head swam giddily as his hands roved over her back, reveling in the classic sculpture of her small waist and the poetic swell of her hips. Then, in a manner that baffled him, there was suddenly nothing between them. The thin fabric seemed magically to evaporate, but he knew that it had fallen at his feet, along with his own covering. The moan in her throat shortened into a rapid, definite rhythm to which her driving body kept perfect time against his.

"God … Karel."

"Dick …" She touched him. "Do you mind …"

"No … no." Her breasts were fragile porcelain cups from which he drank … such maddening sweetness as he had never imagined. Gradually he went to his knees before her, his thundering heart beating out all other sounds save the deathless, birthless song of all the ages that hummed through her lips, without time, without order, yet lovely beyond description.

She leaned over him, caressing his back with her hair and breasts. Suddenly a cry came from deep within her and a convulsive spasm sent her to her knees, until the thick carpet received them.

Later she lay close to him in the crook of his arm, her breath coming in easy, healthy rhythm. Time... he wondered what time it was, idly, lazily. The sleet rang like tiny shot against the glass of the window and the gas log hissed with reassuring steadiness.

A breast peeped through a mass of black hair with such an irresistible invitation that his lips closed over it, sending a quick tremor through her.

"The carpet is rough, Dick."

"I can fix that." He did.

"Come closer... Ah-h-h. Dick... you're so warm and—" The throaty little moan rose higher... and higher, and she seemed to be steel-muscled, satin-soft, yet as resilient as whalebone.

The sleet pattered unceasingly against the windows, the gas log hissed steadily on while their song rose to thundering heights and then cut sharply off in a fast dying pianissimo.

THE END